RENDOVA

Rendova

A.L. HELLAND

Willamina Studios

Contents

1

And Time Seemed to Freeze

"Hello? Hello, can you hear me?"

Duke fumbled with the earpiece from which he could faintly hear a woman. He pushed it into his ear and winced as the voice came at full volume. "Brandon Tyler-Duke, answer me!"

"Goodness, Mother, I'm right here," he said. "Something wrong?"

"This whole thing seems wrong," she complained. "I've got about a dozen messages from some fool who thinks he can grow rhubarb in basalt rock, and you're not here to politely listen and send him away."

"You have to do your work yourself?" Duke asked teasingly.

"That's what my PA is for," she retorted. Her voice softened to a more motherly tone. "How's it going up there? How's your father doing?"

Duke chuckled. "Patience, Mother. I'm not even inside yet."

"I can't wait to see him. I can't believe he's finally coming home," she said dreamily. "Are you still on the ship?"

"I'm in the hatch, which is basically a box between the ship and the station. I'm still waiting for Father and the others to let me in. Is Mr. Channyng with you? You should ask him what the delay is all about."

"Let me find him. I'll be right back."

Her voice was replaced by quiet static. Duke pulled the earpiece out, letting it dangle over the front of his uniform. Pacing over to the window, he rapped his knuckles against the specialty glass in appreciation. It was all that separated him from the black canvas of space. In the very corner of the window he could see the Earth below him, blindingly bright due to the angle of the sun. The window stretched from the floor to the ceiling, taking up an entire wall in the tiny room.

Duke had been on this space station once before, a year earlier. On that occasion the Space Agency had let him accompany a routine inspection so he could visit his father. On that trip, Duke had stood out from the others. While they were astrophysicists and inspectors, with their hands full of scientific instruments and government-regulated supplies, he had walked in as a nineteen-year-old with a potted plant and instructions on how to care for it. His father and the other astronauts had accepted it gratefully, and Duke had gone home pleased.

Duke worked for the Space Agency as a personal assistant to his mother in the Agriculture department. Usually, that meant he sat in front of a computer screen and created simulations of crops on distant planets. Space stations had no need for agriculture, so his trips here were pretty much vacations.

His parents, the Tyler-Dukes, were both longtime members of the SA; his father had been on this station for nearly three years, but today his period was over and he was going back to Earth.

He heard a faint voice from the earpiece, so he shoved it back into his ear. "Hello?"

"Duke, I'm going to ask you to keep your earpiece in." It was Channyng, the supervisor of this particular visit. He referred to him as simply Duke, which was a common nickname for him among his superiors. What was unusual was the man's worried tone. "Where are you? Are you inside?"

"No," Duke answered, "I'm in the hatch. I got out of our ship just fine, but they haven't actually let me into the station yet."

"They aren't answering my calls, so it's possible something is wrong in there. Stay calm, but be prepared for evacuation. Hopefully it's a faulty radio and nothing more."

"Copy that," said Duke. Though he knew he should probably be panicking, he felt strangely calm. Space was dangerous, yes, and he had always preferred studying wheat and corn over risking his life far away from earth. However, though he had no particular love for space, he had never been afraid of it, either. "Should I try manual entry? Does the door open from this side?"

"It does, but you're not equipped to handle whatever threat we may be dealing with," Channyng answered. "Let me contact the others back on your ship. You're a gardener in space, not the sort of person to deal with a potentially hazardous situation."

"I'm an agriculturist," Duke clarified, though he knew it

was in vain, since Channyng had been calling him a gardener since they met. A low *hiss* caught his attention. The door to the station slid open on its own, revealing an empty passage. "Wait a moment, it's open," he said, stepping towards it. "I don't see anyone, though."

"Stay out!" Channyng ordered. "There could be some kind of leak inside!"

"When did they stop answering their radio?" asked Duke, stepping into the passage.

"Yesterday. They failed to acknowledge my call this morning, but nobody seemed concerned but me. I told them to cancel your trip, but apparently my opinion is nothing around here. It's not like I'm the flight coordinator - oh *wait*, I *am!*"

Duke glanced at a panel on the wall. "There isn't a leak," he said. "All of the air levels are perfectly fine."

"Did you go in? I told you to stay out!" Channyng shouted. "Duke, this is a potentially dangerous situation. Something is preventing the entire crew of that station from contacting us, and we haven't done any kind of investigation yet!"

Duke peered around a corner and his breath caught in his throat. "I found somebody," he croaked. "It's a girl. She's dead."

Channyng's voice exploded in his ear, asking him panicked questions and shouting at the people there with him on Earth. Duke pulled the earpiece out and then dropped onto his knees beside the body. The name *Addison* was embroidered in blue letters on the shoulder of her uniform; she was sitting against the wall, her face ashen and her eyes rolled back. A thin blade protruded from below her ribcage.

"What happened?" Duke murmured, his eyes running over the scene. The hallway was empty: no people, no equipment, nothing except the girl. Her curly hair framed her face, beautiful even in death. He had met Dr. Addison briefly on his last visit. She was a microbiologist, if he remembered correctly.

He lifted the earpiece back in. "I don't know what happened," he said, his voice hollow even to his own ears. "She was stabbed. There's a knife. I think somebody killed her, Channyng."

He could hear the man slap a fist against his desk. "Get out of there! If one of the crew is on a murdering rampage, I don't want our favorite gardener anywhere close."

"Agriculturist," Duke corrected. He stood and walked away, leaving Dr. Addison staring vacantly.

"Are you getting out?" Channyng demanded a moment later. "I'm in contact with your ship and they say you aren't back yet. Do I need to send somebody after you? Hello? Brandon Tyler-Duke! Answer me!"

"Brandon, honey!" His mother's voice joined in. "For goodness' sake, get back to the ship!"

Duke pulled the earpiece out, letting it dangle uselessly. The station seemed to grow quieter the farther he went; step by step, he walked deeper into the vacuum. As he rounded a corner, his heart dropped and time itself seemed to freeze.

A man in his early fifties lay face-down on the floor. On the shoulder of his uniform, beneath a pin with the Space Agency insignia, the name *Tyler-Duke* was embroidered. A pot had fallen off of the desk behind him; it lay shattered on the ground, covering the man's legs with dirt and twigs.

"My father's gone, too," Duke said, his voice as dead as the person before him. He didn't bother putting the earpiece back in. The mouthpiece was still on his collar letting Channyng and his mother hear everything he said. "I'm headed back now. No need to send anyone for me."

He could faintly hear Channyng in the earpiece, extending his condolences and promising a thorough investigation, and his mother, hyperventilating. He wrapped his fist around it, muting the sound. With his free hand, he pulled off his father's SA pin and he held it to his chest. Silently he turned his back on the body and made his way down the hallway. He was passing Dr. Addison when a scream echoed through the station.

The confusion of the next few moments was something he would ponder for years to come. The horror was something he would try to forget.

Out of nowhere, the station shook with an explosion, and what felt like a wall of fire and acid swept onto him, flinging him against the wall. There was intense, overwhelming pain. He lost his vision and hearing and for a brief, sickening moment he was convinced he was dead. He felt hands grabbing at him, and he felt the floor slipping away beneath him. A door slammed. Instantly his senses returned, and he found himself sprawled out on the floor of the hatch between the ship and the station where he had been minutes earlier.

As he jumped to his feet, red lights flashed above him and the floor shook. He looked down at his hands and realized with horror that his father's pin was gone. The other door opened, and a medic rushed out and dragged him back onto the ship. Duke was met with complete chaos. Channyng was yelling over their radio too, and the captain was barking orders. Debris from the space station struck their ship, causing the walls to tremble.

"What happened?" Duke gasped, as the young medic pushed him into a chair and covered him with a shock blanket.

"The station exploded," the medic answered. "We don't know why, yet. The doctor will be here in a moment. What happened to your eyes?"

Duke blinked. "There's nothing wrong with my eyes! Who got me out?"

"I did," the medic answered. "I had to drag you. The force of the explosion must have stunned you, even where you were in the hatch."

"The hatch? I wasn't in the hatch, I was in the station."

The young medic shook her head. "Kid, just relax. You might be concussed."

"I was in the station," Duke repeated. "Who got me out of the station?"

"Listen, Mr. Tyler-Duke," the medic said, trying to keep her patience, "if you went into the station, you would be very dead right now."

A doctor came up, and the medic began a whispered conference with him about concussions and mental confusion. Duke hugged the blanket and pulled it over his head. The doctor tried asking him questions but Duke ignored him. He knew they were probably writing notes about shock and trauma, but he didn't care. He could still feel the explosion in the back of his head, as well as the hands that had come from nowhere and dragged him away. The doctor pricked him with a needle and the ship's chaos faded away. He fell into a forced sleep, where despite the drugs, he relived the explosion a thousand times more.

He woke up on Earth in a hospital room. Physically he was fine; he felt no pain and there were no drugs or IVs in sight. He sat up, clutching the thin blanket against his chest.

"Morning, glory," somebody said, causing Duke to jump. A tall, imposing man stood in the doorway, wearing a dark suit paired with an obnoxious tie. Duke knew him slightly: his name was Ernest Valentine, and he was a prominent member of the Space Agency. But since Duke worked in Agriculture and Valentine was in the Legal department, they never had much reason to talk.

"What are you doing here?" Duke asked. He knew he looked weak, huddled on a bed with a blanket, so he tried putting some authority into his voice. "Where's Channyng?"

Valentine swaggered in, his hands in his pockets. "Channyng's on his way. You've been out for twelve hours, by the way."

"What happened? Why did the space station explode?"

Valentine shrugged. "We don't know for sure. The cover story I was given is that the residents were involved in inter-space smuggling and got into a fight, and with how bad that sounds, the real story must be a doozy. Nobody knows the details, though, except the higher ups. That's the way of these things: secrets, secrets. As usual, I have my job cut out for me, making us look good to the public." He leaned his shoulder against the wall, hovering over the bed. "By the way, I heard you claimed you went into the station. Not even Channyng knows what you're talking about. You were actually in the hatch the entire time, I'm told."

"I was on the station," Duke insisted, half-heartedly. "I walked out of the hatch and went inside, and I found Addison and my father. And then there was an explosion, though apparently it should've killed me."

"Maybe it did," said Valentine.

Duke gave a bitter laugh. "What on earth do you mean by that?"

"Something happened to you," said Valentine, "And it's different from what happened to the rest of the world. There is something impossible going on here, Mr. Tyler-Duke. Look." He pushed a machine towards the bed. It was a heart rate monitor, with a dark, lifeless screen. "It'll be hard to see, but I want you to take a look at your reflection."

Duke squinted. He could make out the outline of his face: a strong jaw, cheekbones, a headful of chestnut hair. For a moment, he noticed nothing strange. But then his eyes met his own and a startled cry escaped him. He remembered the young medic asking about his eyes, and now he understood. His mild, brown eyes were gone, replaced with orbs of fire. The whites of his eyes were still there, as well as his pupils, but the iris had been replaced by a fiery orange band that flickered and reflected brightly off the monitor.

Channyng burst into the room, his features drawn in consternation. "Duke!" he exclaimed. "You're alive! Thank goodness you never left the hatch!"

"I *did* leave the hatch. I went into the station!"

"You never went into the station. I was afraid you'd be like this, the doctors gave me an entire list of your erratic behavior. They also said something about your eyes." He stepped closer, studying Duke's face. "They were right! It's like fire... that's not natural!"

"The doctors found some unrecognizable signals coming from his brain scan," said Valentine quietly. "There is something very unnatural going on here."

All color drained from Channyng's face. "The station ignoring my calls, an unexplained explosion, and now this! Make the doctors sign a non-disclosure, Valentine, and Duke, keep quiet about this. This is an Agency secret until we know more about it."

"Yes sir," Duke said miserably.

"I agree," said Valentine, straightening his tie. "I'm going to have a hard enough time making us look good after the explosion. We don't need more mysteries to throw at the public. We'll have to watch you for any disturbing... side effects. I'll see you around, Tyler-Duke. Mr. Channyng." He nodded a farewell and stepped out.

Channyng waved a finger at Duke. "Stop telling people you were in the explosion! I don't want you in the psychiatric ward. I'm expecting you in my office first thing in the morning."

"Mother is expecting me at Agriculture! And whether or not I went into the station, my father is dead, isn't he? Don't I get a day off?"

"Your mom is on leave, but you can forget it. This isn't just hard on you, this is hard on everyone involved. I'm pulling you out of Agriculture for now. You're my personal assistant until we sort everything out."

Duke opened his mouth to protest but then shut it. Channyng was halfway out the door before Duke finally spoke up.

"I went onto the station. I really did."

Channyng shook his head and walked out.

October 2, 2244 - "...This is Patricia Mays, and I'm here with the Head of Public Relations for the SA. Is it true that there are no survivors from the unexpected explosion of the Astrum X?" "Unfortunately that is true. We will be holding a public memorial service for the seven astronauts who lost their lives today..."

October 3 - "It is not the intention of this column to criticize the work of this city's beloved Space Agency. However, we can't help but question how an explosion of this magnitude was possible. If the Agency actually followed the standard safety regulations, we must ask - would seven people be alive today?"

October 3 - "At the press conference directly following the explosion of the Astrum X, the Head of PR was seen to grow visibly agitated when a news anchor asked about a popular rumor. The rumor is that the Space Agency is storing nuclear weapons on space stations that would be illegal on the soil of most countries. It is arguable that a space station holds Nova Atlantis immunity..."

October 7 - "This is Patricia Mays, bringing you the latest from Nova Atlantis. The memorial for the astronauts who lost their lives in the explosion of the Astrum X went without a hitch until a son of one of the victims, Brandon Tyler-Duke, 19, was given the mic. He appeared to have an alteration to his eyes that we've never seen before, which makes them shine with an unnatural orange light. He started reading a pre-written tribute, but was interrupted by his mother, the well-known scientist Dr. Tyler-Duke. She was obviously beside herself with grief, and made claims such as 'nobody is telling me the truth,' and 'my husband is dead, and now they're doing things to my son.' Brandon attempted to stop her. Watch what happened next..."

October 21 - "The Tyler-Dukes have become infamous in the wake of the Astrum X's explosion. After the circus that was the memorial, they were seen together at a press conference at the SA complex. In front of dozens of reporters and cameras, Dr. Tyler-Duke told her son: 'your father was so proud when you started working with me, because he knew you'd be a scientist. But the moment he's dead you quit and now you're debasing yourself as a PA!' Brandon, 19, responded in an angry tone with: 'for goodness' sake, mother, give it a rest. Don't use my father's death as an excuse to get what you want!' 'That's not what I'm doing,' she responded. 'That's what Channyng's doing. He's an incompetent fool and I don't want you associating with him. It was his job to bring your father home... how did that end?'"

Channyng swept into his office, where Duke was waiting, studying an electronic tablet. "I think I have a good shot at promotion," Channyng announced, dropping into his swivel chair. "It would be a lot easier, though, if my PA would stop yelling at his mother."

"I'm sorry, sir," Duke said, his shoulders drooping. "She makes me so angry."

"Hopefully Public Relations can find something else to distract the media with," Channyng mused. "I really need people to like us." He smiled wryly. "At least we have attention."

Duke sighed, dropping his gaze to look at his tablet. His face pinched when he saw his fingers. "Sir... my hands are glowing!"

Channyng's eyes snapped up. Duke's hands were wrapped with a transparent fire, and he began to fade from sight. He dropped the tablet and it hit the tile floor with a *crack*. With wide eyes, Duke reached for the older man, but before he could touch him he vanished.

Jumping to his feet, Channyng grabbed the broken tablet and looked around wildly. He was grabbing the door to call for help when the transparent flames returned, and with them Duke, who solidified on shaky legs.

"Sir," he gasped, "I... I think I can time-travel."

Channyng's eyes narrowed and he slammed the door. "Don't," he said with emphasis, "tell anyone."

2

The Space Agency

Ten years later, shortly after President Johnson of Reka II had been arrested...

Duke scanned his badge on the meeting room door, and it unlocked and swung open. He stepped into the familiar room. A round table took up most of the space, and the Heads of the Space Agency were taking their seats around it. Most of them ignored his presence, though he got a slight nod from Ernest Valentine. Since the explosion of the space station, Valentine had moved from Legal to Public Relations, and now served as the Head of that department.

Duke's mother, Dr. Tyler-Duke, was in her chair flipping through her tablet. Her hair was a bit of a mess and her face lifts were getting obvious, but even at her age she was still the Head of Agriculture. She barely looked up as he entered.

Channyng, like Valentine, had been promoted. He had been elected as president of the SA. As his PA, Duke took a seat next to him, folded his hands and waited. The others were chatting, killing time while waiting for those who were running late. Having been on Reka mere hours earlier, Duke found their chatter frivolous. They had always been like this, he recalled. The sky could be falling, but the Space Agency would sip their coffees and chat about how it wasn't really their fault.

The door opened and a man swept in, taking a seat behind his nameplate reading *Dr. E. A. Moon.* Skipping any kind of greeting, he plowed over the chit-chat of the others. "I believe we should turn to the subject at hand," he said. Everyone fell silent as he continued with the intensity of a lawyer. "Mr. Duke, what was the condition of Reka II when you last saw it?"

He stood up. "Reka II was in a famine for months," he began. "We shut the force field down, which let in the *Kenswick*, which has enough food to last the survivors until more ships can arrive. When I left, Johnson was in custody, and Ivan Koswitch was overseeing the distribution of food and supplies."

As he sat down, his mother raised her hand. "The Captain of the *Kenswick* sent in his report. He stayed in the colony for a week. I'll read a few lines."

Dr. Moon gave a brief nod and she lifted her tablet. "I quote: 'Reka II is recovering but still in chaos. My ship alleviated the threat of hunger, but during the famine, water systems, electric lines, government and other factors had been shut down. There were several casualties from sickness and the cold. Some perished in the snow while searching for fuel for their cars. One of the towns, Kingstown, heard of how the president cheated them of food during the famine, and that led to several riots. I helped as much as I could before starting for Earth.'"

"And where were you, Mr. Duke?" interrupted Moon. "Why didn't you stay and help the Rekans?"

Duke winced. "Why would I?" he asked. "Channyng asked me to investigate Johnson, so I did. I wasn't really there in a professional role. I thought the crew of the *Kenswick* had everything under control."

Dr. Simons, an Asian-Indian man with a habit of stressing his words, spoke up. "But *how* did you get to Reka II in the *first* place? I looked at the records of our latest ships, and I have yet to find your name. You have an *uncanny* way of getting around, Mr. Duke."

Channyng thankfully intervened.

"Has this meeting really become about what my PA does on his time off?" he asked with a chuckle. "Dr. Simons, we have real issues to discuss today." He kept smiling, but his voice dropped to a more sinister tone. "And you'd best be careful of what you say about Mr. Duke. As we all know, anybody who messes with him, messes with me."

Several of the people present gave nervous laughs. Channyng said it like a joke, but everyone knew that with the kind of power the man had, it was anything but. Dr. Simons shot a suspicious look towards Duke, but wisely dropped the subject.

"Well then," Dr. Moon resumed. "I suppose we ought to discuss President Johnson. From what I've heard, we supposedly believe him to be a time-traveler?"

Channyng nodded amiably. "Did you get a chance to read the written brief my team sent out? We included indisputable evidence. His fingerprints are literally a ninety-eight percent match of Teddy Reka's from over fifty years ago."

"Maybe we can accept it as a working hypothesis," Moon relented. "But you're claiming that Teddy Johnson, a madman from two hundred years ago, somehow rewired his watch and set himself up in our century as a president. I believe the man has serious issues, but I wouldn't take it that far. Nobody that we know of is capable of time-travel."

"Like you said, let's take it as a working hypothesis," Channyng said. "I believe he founded the colony as Teddy Reka in the past, and then time-traveled into our time when it was more stable, and knocked off our previous administration so he could rule instead. He then set up an illegal force field and sent us false reports."

Dr. Simons joined in. "He's been *deceiving* us for a *long* time. Fifty *years* ago, the previous administration of this Agency chose Reka II to be the *first* colonized planet. Teddy Reka was the man who pushed for it, and if Channyng is right, Teddy Reka and Johnson are the same man."

"I'm right," Channyng yawned, locking his fingers together behind his head and leaning back.

Dr. Moon rose to his feet. "I suggest we shut down Reka II." He sat back down.

The room went quiet. Around the table, eyebrows were raised in shock or lowered in aversion. Channyng sat up and shook his head. "But Dr. Moon, we've poured a huge amount of our resources into this. And what would it look like to the public if we shut down our very first attempt at a space colony?"

"Space is unsafe," Dr. Moon said simply. "We would be wise to let the public know it."

"But *really*, Dr. Moon," said Dr. Simon, "you *can't* expect us to throw away our hard *work*."

Dr. Moon leaned back in his chair, and gazed at the man across from him through dark, half-closed eyes. "Does Mr. Valentine have anything to say?"

Dr. Tyler-Duke sighed, slamming her tablet down. "Mr. Valentine disagrees with you very eloquently," she declared, "And now we should break for lunch."

A chorus of snickers and whispered *bravos* went through the room and Channyng glared at everybody until they were quiet. Dr. Moon almost smirked.

Mr. Valentine rose to his feet with his never-ending smile; a smile that looked good for publicity, but Duke often doubted the sincerity behind it. "Dr. Tyler-Duke, I must apologize if I've gotten into the habit of disagreeing with our dear Moon every time he speaks. And yes, I'm long-winded. But we must have a devil's advocate, mustn't we? I know what you're thinking: we must have our lunch, too, and old Valentine looks ready to talk his head off. Don't worry. I only have a few things to say."

Duke's mother didn't look convinced, but she kept quiet.

Valentine continued. "Friends, colleagues, before us we have some rather important decisions. We can fight or we can put up the white flag. We can push forward or fall back. Dr. Moon suggests we choose to retreat. I must ask you: are we men of science and exploration or are we cowards?

"Reka II is in chaos, but we always knew that might happen. We counted the cost, didn't we? Any new venture in Space is dangerous, which is why we huddle here in this great city and consult with our scientists and engineers day by day. Most of us were not here for that decision fifty years ago to colonize Reka, but we've all put blood, sweat and tears into it since then.

"Dr. Simons, you designed the newer layout of the Base. Dr. Tyler-Duke, you worked on crop production. Dr. Moon, you yourself put in countless hours supervising the shipment of food and top grade medical supplies. This is a work we have made with our own hands. This is also a dream mankind has been dreaming since the beginning of time."

He put his hands on the table and leaned forward. "When it comes to President Johnson, nothing has been proven. Sure, he time-travels, but it's never been done before so we've never regulated it, so I'm guessing it's not a crime. Even if he is not the man we thought he was, is that Reka's fault? The scientists and military there didn't vote him in. Neither did the civilians, who, if I can remind you, were refugees fleeing the turmoil across the Atlantic. It was our decision to send him there."

Duke's mother was beginning to fidget, so Valentine shot her a smile. "I won't bother you much longer with my thoughts, except this: was our colony to blame for the disaster, or a series of unfortunate - but avoidable - events? Even if you blame Johnson, he's out of the picture. Captain Riley has him in the *Kenswick* as we speak, and they're already in orbit.

"And Reka? I believe they're holding their breath, wondering what our verdict will be. These are refugees who have finally found a home. Scientists who have found a job. Will we sympathize with them and help them back onto their feet, or drag them to earth and forget our vision, the glory of space? There is much more to be said, but now you're familiar with my position."

Valentine took his seat. Before Dr. Tyler-Duke could call for a lunch break, Dr. Moon fired off a question. "Mr. Valentine, are you aware of how long the journey from Reka to Earth is?"

"Something close to two months, I believe," he answered.

"Sixty-two days and twelve hours," Dr. Moon said. "Not to mention forty minutes. And are you aware of the fact that our communication system is hardly reliable? It is sketchy, if I may say so. How many times have we heard a direct message from the colony?"

"I believe the radio worked only once," Valentine admitted. "Dr. Simons, you designed it, didn't you?"

Simons, the Indian man, drew himself up. "Yes, I did," he said, stressing his words. "And *sketchy* is hardly the term I would use for it. Are you aware of how many *hundreds* of *thousands* of kilometers I'm trying to beam *radio* waves? I'd like to see you try, if you're going to call my work *sketchy*."

"Forgive me," shrugged Dr. Moon, as if he didn't really

care much about being forgiven. "But Mr. Valentine, do you really believe Johnson was not to blame? And if we put another tyrant over these colonists, are we to call that sympathy? They are *hundreds* of *thousands* of kilometers away and we *cannot* even contact them with Dr. Simon's *superior* technology. If we leave Reka standing, we'd only be giving it a chance to go through the fire once more."

Dr. Simons looked offended at the impersonation, while Valentine looked thoughtful. "I see your point," the latter said. "Maybe we need to implement a different sort of government, but we can't give it up completely. Friends, we're the Space Agency. If we can't colonize Space, we might as well go home. But I think we can give it another shot."

"Dr. Moon, Mr. Valentine, this has all been very interesting," said Dr. Tyler-Duke. "I hate to interrupt, but we knew this would be a short meeting. With the upcoming demonstration this week, we have to put Reka on the back burner for now."

Duke looked up sharply. "Reka is more important, isn't it? Even forgetting the famine, I witnessed an entirely unheard of phenomenon on their Red Planet that needs to be addressed!"

"Why don't you stay quiet until someone asks for your opinion, Brandon?" his mother asked, an edge to her voice.

Duke's eyes glimmered with the promise of anger. "I believe I have a right to voice my opinions here, mother. Not only have I served at the SA for longer than most of the people here, but I know more about the Reka colony right now than anyone else in the Agency."

He felt Channyng's hand on his arm, an unspoken command to hush. Dr. Tyler-Duke's mouth curled in a sneer. "I don't care that you're the president's pet, Brandon. I got to this table by hard work."

"Please, this is unnecessary," Channyng intervened. "Duke, you want to take care of Reka, and I appreciate that. But the demonstration this week does take the highest priority. Dr. Tyler-Duke, how is the chemical display coming along?"

Her sour mood hung over her like a stormcloud, but she forced an arrogant smile. "It's coming along nicely," she said. "We're scheduled to test it down in the bay tomorrow."

"Wonderful, wonderful," Channyng said, though his attempt at clearing the air with his cheerfulness was about as effective as throwing an air freshener into a burning building. "We all have places to be, so I'll bid you adieu. And to all of you preparing the demonstration, good luck!"

Chairs squeaked and tablets hummed into sleep mode as people stood up. Valentine stood and approached Dr. Moon for a handshake, but the doctor clutched his binder and brushed past him, ignoring the outstretched hand.

Dr. Tyler-Duke tucked her tablet under her arm and strutted out, ignoring her son and everyone else. Channyng waved a finger at Duke. "Don't fight with her. We've been through this time and time again."

"I'm sorry," Duke said, running his hands through his hair. "She makes me so angry sometimes."

"You did disown her in public."

"She disowned me in public!"

"After you called her a poor excuse for a scientist. Also in public."

Duke sighed. "I didn't mean it. She always started it."

"There are still clips circulating the internet of your shouting matches. Man, how long ago was all of that anyway?"

"Ten years since the explosion," Duke said wearily.

"I sympathize with you, man, but you gotta move on, you and your mom." Channyng grabbed his travel mug, taking a sip. "Anyway, about your mission. Good job, but I want you to put aside the Reka case for now."

Duke's eyes widened. "But…"

"Shh!" Channyng glanced at the stragglers, still collecting their things and chatting. "I know I said you could do time-travel work for me, but now I'm afraid it's too much. If Dr. Simons is looking into how you get around, that means we've been too obvious. The man isn't even bright. I don't want anyone else to get suspicious, and you have plenty of work to do in my office anyway."

"I've been sending your emails and scheduling your meetings for a decade now," Duke said, his eyes flaring up. "I could be in Agriculture right now like I always wanted, but ever since we found out I could time-travel you've said there has to be something better for me. So, what is it? A promotion to fetching coffee?"

"We've been over this time and time again," Channyng groaned. "We need to be careful. I want to use your powers, I really do, but I don't want to lose them, either. People already don't like you, so imagine what would happen if anybody found out. I'm the only thing keeping you safe here, so give me a break, man."

Duke sighed, standing up. "I'm sorry, I'm sorry. I should probably go home and rest. Need anything before I go?"

"I have coffee, thanks," he said drily. "I'm not helpless. By the way, who's your friend in the lobby? Boring face, black jacket?"

"Someone's in the lobby?"

"Uh-huh," Channyng said. "I told you, no time-traveling if you're gonna bring back strays. Don't endanger time. Put him back."

"His name is King, and I'm sorry, I will. Goodbye sir."

Duke headed for the exit. Valentine met him at the door as if he'd been waiting for him. "What do you think of Moon?" he asked casually, his hands in his pockets.

"I'm sorry, is there something I can do for you? I was about to head home," Duke said, reaching for the door.

"We should talk more, you and I. I think you're wasted on Channyng."

"When you become president, give me a call."

"Hey." Valentine grabbed his arm, jerking him to a stop. The others in the room pretended not to notice, carrying on their conversations and sipping their drinks. "We haven't spoken in a while. I've noticed that the last few years have been rough on you, eh?"

"Let go of me."

Valentine tightened his grip, and Duke's eyes blazed in warning. The man leaned towards his ear, dropping his voice to a whisper. "Choose your enemies wisely, son, but more importantly be sure of your friends. I'm just trying to warn you."

"Of what?"

"I've got three words. Johnson is free."

Channyng walked up. "Trouble, Duke?"

Valentine let him go abruptly, leaving him to stumble against the wall. "We were just catching up," the man said with one of his famous publicity smiles.

Channyng nodded, unconvinced. "Come on, Valentine. I've got a few notes about the press conference this weekend that I'd like to go over with you."

He ushered the man out quickly, leaving Duke alone.

<h1 style="text-align:center">3</h1>

<h1 style="text-align:center">Nova Atlantis</h1>

Out in the lobby, Jett King sat in a corner, waiting. He had never liked skyscrapers, and this one was no exception. It was only a small part of what Duke had called the SA complex, a large, sprawling group of connected buildings. So far in this century Jett had seen Reka, a distant, struggling colony with the bare necessities. Now he was in Nova Atlantis, a city named after the legendary utopia, and so far it lived up to its name. It was his first real glimpse of Earth in the future.

An entire wall was made up of a window with a wide view of the city. Blue, glass-like material formed into passages on the ground with trains whooshing through them. The passages went through buildings in some places, and in other places they rose up into bridges.

Jett also had a clear view of the ocean. Bridges, all made out of the blue glass, were stacked several stories high across the bay and outflowing river. The sun shone on the glass and the ocean, lighting them up with the same brilliant blue. Several gulls flew by, headed toward the sea. Being from an inland state, Jett had never seen the ocean in person. Roads and tunnels began at the beach and then pointed inland.

There were skyscrapers, all set on a carpet of bright green grass. Each building was a magnificent shape - smooth ovals, triangles, solid cubes - and each one was blue and glittering. They were connected with passages and trains, some of which were suspended in the air between higher floors.

Nova Atlantis was beautiful, and from what Jett had heard, it was essentially a research center the size of a city.

The door to the meeting room opened, and over the next few minutes Jett watched a variety of people trickle out. Some of them went into the elevator, some of them went down the hall. A tall man with an obnoxious tie swaggered out with his hands in his pockets, talking to a man with Asian features and a crocodile leather suit jacket. Moments after them, Duke stumbled out, looking flustered.

"Come on," he said, heading towards the elevator.

"What's the matter?" Jett asked.

Duke pulled him into the elevator and the doors slid shut. Despite them being alone, he dropped his voice to a whisper. "Somebody told me Johnson is free."

"What?" Jett said blankly. "How is that possible?"

"I don't know, I don't even know if it's true. But I'm going to find out."

"You said earlier that the *Kenswick* hasn't even landed yet."

Duke ran his hands through his hair. "That's what I was told."

Jett always felt sick in elevators, and a futuristic one, like the skyscraper, was no exception. He was glad when they reached the bottom. Stepping out, he hurried after Duke through the front doors. Duke seemed to know his way around Nova Atlantis well, and for that Jett was thankful. He had rarely left the small town of Angel in his lifetime, so here in a sprawling, futuristic hub of science he was completely lost.

He wondered if the rest of his friends felt as overwhelmed as he did. Since Duke didn't want to bring everyone into the SA complex, Dr. Emmett, Robbie, Parker, Cariss, and Tate had been dropped off at Duke's house. Jett hoped they were taking advantage of the free time to rest up. Since they had time-traveled, they had all been on Reka mere hours earlier.

Duke led Jett onto a platform that was made of the same blue material as everything else. Warning lights flashed and a train whooshed in. It wasn't anything like the trains Jett had seen before, but it was all he knew to compare it to. A holographic screen came up, detailing what route the train would take next. Jett stared at it, trying to make sense of the technology. He was rudely interrupted by Duke, who grabbed his arm and dragged him into the train before they missed it.

With a barely audible *hiss* the train took off. To Jett, it felt more like flying than anything else. Most of his fellow passengers wore suits, and Jett guessed they were all on their way to different meetings with different agencies. When they saw Duke, some gaped at him openly, while others whispered and tried to point discreetly. The words *"fiery eyes"* and *"Channyng's PA"* were passed around. Surprisingly, it didn't seem to faze Duke at all.

The train stopped so smoothly that Jett wouldn't have

noticed if Duke hadn't grabbed his arm again. They were the only ones to step out. The doors shut behind them and the train *hissed* and took off.

They found themselves on a deserted station which Jett recognized as his very first view of the city. That morning, they had landed the *Starlight* and had walked to this very station to board a train to Duke's house. A metal walkway led to the Space Agency's docking bay, which was a vast yard full of test ships, ships under maintenance, and ships in storage. If he squinted, Jett could see Robbie's *Starlight* glinting in the sun on the far end.

"Jett, look. Is that smoke?" Duke asked, pointing.

Shielding his eyes from the sun, he followed Duke's gaze. Past the docking bay, there were miles and miles of nothing but brownish hills. It was a stark contrast to Nova Atlantis behind them, shining like a blue jewel set in a carpet of green. The stretch before them was bare, almost a desert.

It didn't take long to find what Duke was pointing at. A column of smoke rose up to the sky, surrounded by several helicopters and drones. Flashing red and blue lights surrounded the scene, but it was too distant to see what had happened.

"You don't suppose..." Duke started, but his voice trailed off.

His watch beeped. He had a large, square-faced watch, which besides the time-travel features he had added to it, he used for a variety of things: phone calls, paying money, and searching the internet. It reminded Jett of the smart-watch his wife Maddie used to have before she died.

Duke lifted his wrist. "Yes, Channyng?"

A voice that Jett assumed to be Channyng answered. "I'm about to give you information that we're keeping to a need-to-know basis."

The fire in Duke's eyes rolled in agitation. "What is it? Why didn't you tell me at the complex?"

"I didn't want to risk it. I don't want people to overhear and start mass hysteria. Apparently, directly before our meeting, the *Kenswick* crash-landed east of Nova Atlantis. There were three casualties and they're still assessing the injuries. During the confusion, Johnson escaped."

Jett stared at the column of smoke, while Duke pressed a hand to his face. Channyng's voice continued.

"We've alerted Security throughout the city, and I'm confident he'll be apprehended shortly, but in the meantime he could pose a danger to you. You were responsible for his arrest, so there's no knowing what Johnson would do if he were to find you. Only the Heads and Security are supposed to know this, so don't let on that I told you."

"Thank you, Channyng," Duke said, trying to steady his voice. "What do you want me to do?"

"You know we can't have anything distracting us from the demonstration this week," he said, "So catching him can't be our highest priority. Wait patiently and keep your eyes open. I'll let you know if anything happens."

"Ask about the Rekan passengers," said Jett.

"What happened to the Rekan passengers?" Duke echoed.

There was a moment's pause. "I'd almost forgotten there were Rekans on board. I'll certainly ask about them."

"Are they all alive?"

"I can't say. I'd better arrange medical treatment if any of them need it."

"One of them is named Anton Venedict, and he's not actually a Rekan, but a boy Johnson brought with him from the 21st century," Duke said. "I've been trying to bring him back."

"I'll take care of it," Channyng promised. "See ya, Duke."

The call ended and Duke dropped his wrist to his side. "Let's get back into town," he said, starting a brisk walk to the empty station. Jett turned his back on the column of smoke and flashing lights and followed him.

4

Alone in a Crowd

That night, Jett found himself in a large, quiet house that Duke said was his. Jett knew that Duke was from this century (the 23rd), and he was beginning to realize that the man's life was still devoted to it. In the living room, there were several boxes in the corner full of wires and equipment like the boxes Duke had in his office in Nebraska.

There was a lonely easy-chair which Jett quickly settled down in. He had just finished saying goodnight to the others. He guessed that other people used to live here with Duke, since there were three bedrooms, and he had called them "mine, my parents', and the guestroom." Cariss and Parker were in one, while Tate and Dr. Emmett had taken the other.

Duke was at the Space Agency again, but he had insisted that Jett join the others at his house for the night. Robbie was upstairs in the attic, and Jett had been planning to spend the night there too, but all of a sudden he felt too tired to move. It felt like years had passed since he had sat in an easy-chair. His eyelids began to droop, and he had the funny sensation of being magnetized to the chair.

He jumped when the front door opened, wondering if he'd fallen asleep. Duke stepped in, shaking water off his suit and wiping his shoes on the doormat.

"Is it raining?" Jett asked in surprise.

"Yes. The weather changes quickly here, and it rains a lot."

Jett sat up and rubbed his eyes. "Any news?"

"Anton's alive," Duke answered, and Jett let out a breath he hadn't realized he was holding. "And apparently there were quite a few Rekans on the *Kenswick*. One is Anton, of course, and then there were eight or nine others. One of them is Ivan Koswitch."

"Ivan?" Jett repeated. His mind darted back to the bearded, desperate vice president. "I thought he was left in charge of Reka."

"The *Kenswick's* captain told me that Ivan asked for a ride back to Earth after we had left. Ivan and his friends have taken up temporary residence here in Nova Atlantis. But there still isn't a trace of Johnson." He sank into a folding chair. There were no couches or anything in the room, and Jett felt bad for being in the only comfortable seat, but he was far too tired to get up.

"Where's Anton?" he asked. "If he's missing, we're back where we started."

Duke grimaced at the thought. "Anton's in the hospital," he said. "I stopped by on my way back and saw him."

"Is he okay?"

"Mostly. He got second degree burns and a touch of whiplash, I'm told, but they'll let him out tomorrow morning."

His words dragged, and for the first time Jett noticed that

his face was pale and drawn. He wondered if Duke was one of those polite hosts who stayed up until all his guests were in bed, and he decided he probably was. Though every muscle in his body protested, Jett pulled himself to his feet. "I'm going to get some sleep. We can see Anton tomorrow, right?"

"Maybe. It all depends on what Channyng says."

"Who's Channyng?"

"He's the president of the Space Agency," Duke said dismissively.

"Do you work for him? I know you said you did time-travel work for the Agency."

The fire in his eyes began to move moodily. "I might have been too sure of myself. Can I get you anything before you go to bed?"

"Do you never sleep? I'm pretty certain you didn't sleep last night," Jett said. He knew it was random, but Duke looked committed to sitting on the folding chair staring at his watch all night.

"I'm not sure I've slept since we've met," Duke said, laughing without any humor. "I can take care of myself, King." He looked down at his watch.

Realizing that the conversation was over, Jett shook his head and trudged up the stairs. On the second floor, he opened a narrow door and walked up another flight of stairs to the attic. Robbie was sprawled out on a sleeping bag, asleep. He hadn't bothered to crawl in and was still wearing his boots.

Jett unrolled a sleeping bag for himself and laid it out on the floor. As he pulled his shoes off, a wave of homesickness swept over him. He was lost. He knew he was in Nova

Atlantis, but those words didn't mean anything to him. His routine was broken. Every night he put his shoes in the same corner and threw his jacket over the same chair; after tucking Logan in, he would sit in his easy-chair with a mug of tea and talk with Teddy, either in person or over the phone. He was not just a creature of habit, he realized: he anchored himself in it. Ever since his wife Maddie had died Jett had spent his life avoiding change.

He buried his face in his sleeping bag and shuddered. Somewhere in his mind he felt alarmed at his own behavior, and he tried to gain control of himself. Holding back tears that threatened to spill, he forced himself to breathe in and out, and after several agonizing minutes the desire to cry died away. He was left listening to the silence that was somehow so different from the silence at home.

There was nothing he could do. For once in his life, he could not find anything familiar to hide himself behind. Maddie was gone. Teddy was gone. Angel, Nebraska had opened up, letting in a whole new world of time-travel and strangers. He had fought against change and he had lost.

5

Sabotage

The next morning, Duke slipped out before any of the others were awake and made his way to the SA complex. As he walked in, automated sensors picked up his movement and the lights flickered on in every hallway he went through. They shut off behind him, since it was too early for them to stay on full-time. He passed several offices with empty chairs and quiet desks, and then the elevator brought him to an upper floor where he sought out a door that said *President's Office: L. A. Channyng.*

He stepped inside. The desk was mahogany, and it matched the shelves along the wall showcasing expensive trinkets and a pitcher with matching tumblers. Channyng himself was across the room, juggling his tablet, jacket, and a disposable cup of coffee. "Good morning, Duke," he said cheerfully, dropping his things onto the desk. "You look like you haven't slept in a week. How are you?"

"I'm all right," he answered. He lifted his watch and navigated to the on-screen calendar. "Can we go over my schedule? You keep changing it last minute and I'm not entirely sure of what I'm supposed to be working on, since you want me to drop Reka and all."

"That was the most passive aggressive thing I've ever heard you say," Channyng chuckled. "Put your watch down. I've got a question for you." He reached for the bookshelf and retrieved a small paperback, which he promptly slapped onto the desk. "Have you ever read this?"

Duke scanned the cover. "'*Angel's Crypt: A Publication of the Riddles*,'" he read aloud. "I've never heard of it. I don't read novels."

"It's not a novel. This book is almost two hundred years old," Channyng said, picking it up and flipping through the pages. "Not this copy, of course, but the riddles themselves. It's not as popular as it once was, but it's always been a favorite among treasure seekers. Now, this is gonna sound like a non sequitur, but I saw your friend in the hallway yesterday. Black jacket, boring face - that one. Anyway, I thought I recognized him, and sure enough, look at this. This is one of the original illustrations."

He turned the book towards Duke. On the page was the head and shoulders of a man who looked very much like Jett King. The drawing had been sketched with a pen or pencil and then copied and printed in black ink. The man's face was at an angle, smiling at something out of frame, his eyes creased in laughter. The artist had taken great care to keep the plainness and simplicity of Jett's face, but the intense expression in Jett's eyes made the drawing leap off the page.

"Strange, huh?" Channyng said, watching Duke's reaction

closely. "Now, I know you said that this man was from the past, so the logical reason for this is that he wrote the book and included this flattering picture of himself. But do you know why this book used to be so popular? It's because it predicted the future. It talks about a city of glass that housed the best scientists in the world. The clues are vague, so it can be viewed as nothing more than a lucky guess from someone with a wild imagination. But when I was a kid, I was convinced that it was written about a time-traveler from the past who had seen Nova Atlantis."

"Since Jett has seen Nova Atlantis, it's possible that he was involved in making the book," Duke shrugged. "It's interesting, and I'll definitely take a look into it, but for now I need to hurry and get home. Can we go over the schedule?"

"Duke, this book also talks about Angel's Crypt, which supposedly holds a bridge between worlds. This is even better than the legend of Atlantis. Whoever wrote these riddles hid a treasure trove of innumerable wealth on the brink of a huge, metaphysical discovery, and people have been looking for the place for two hundred years."

"I don't know Jett King very well, but I can assure you he doesn't know anything about hidden treasure," Duke said.

"If he's as boring as he looks, I believe you," Channyng said, studying the picture. "But what about the boy in the hospital, Anton Venedict? Is he related to King somehow?"

"King is his father."

"Huh." Channyng eyed the illustration for a beat longer before snapping the book shut. "Anyway. I want you to bring Jett King and any of his friends that came with him to me before you take them home. To my house, please, not the complex. Now, I've got an update on the *Kenswick*. Valentine and I went to the crash scene last night and we were told it was a clear case of sabotage."

"Sabotage?"

"Somebody managed to switch the fuel lines with the water lines," he explained. "On a freighter that size nearing the end of a two-month trip, a lot of people tried to use water. The place was flooded with fuel."

"I would think the sabotager would be worried about killing himself," Duke said.

Channyng shrugged, picking up his coffee. "I don't know what was going through his mind. Whoever did it chose the right moment. The *Kenswick* was already in Earth's atmosphere, a stone's throw away from the docking bay when a fire started. The captain chose to try landing in the hills rather than fly a burning ship into Nova Atlantis."

"I suppose Johnson is one of the suspects," Duke said.

"It doesn't seem like it," Channyng answered. "The remains of his cell have been investigated. He had no access to the fuel lines from there, and there's no way he could have gotten out without anyone knowing. No, I'm afraid we have another person to deal with."

"Ivan Koswitch," Duke suggested. "He didn't seem to get along very well with Johnson, but who knows? Maybe he has a reason to break him out."

Channyng sipped his coffee. "What about Anton Venedict?" he asked carefully.

"I don't think the boy is capable of switching fuel and water lines," Duke said, frowning.

"But it's possible, isn't it? And if he commits a crime here, he has to pay for it here."

"Of course, but…"

"I'm putting him in SA custody."

"He's from the 21st century and his family wants him back, sir," Duke objected.

Channyng held up his hands, shaking his head. "I can talk to his family personally when you bring them over. But remember, Reka is no longer your responsibility."

"But time-travel is, right?" he asked. "If Anton's out of place, that's my responsibility. You said I could start using my powers to help out."

"I said I'd give you a chance and I did. I appreciate the work you put into finding Johnson, but I'd rather you slow down with the time-travel stuff. You're my PA, Duke, and I need you to start acting like it again."

"So what do you want me to do?" he asked wearily.

Before he could answer the door burst open. First rushed in Dr. Moon, the Head of Health and Safety, and behind him swaggered Valentine. They had famous reputations for disagreeing vehemently on everything professional and for hating each other in their personal lives, so it was odd to see them together.

Dr. Moon got straight to the point. "There's been a murder," he announced. "It was Dr. Simons from Communications."

"That's too bad," said Channyng. Neither he nor Duke were very close to the man, but he had been a regular at meetings for many years.

"His body was found down by the coast," Valentine said, folding his arms. "He was shot. It was a laser, not an actual bullet. This was last night, a few hours after the crash of the *Kenswick*."

"Do we have an idea of who did it?" Channyng asked, leaning back in his chair.

"Not officially," said Dr. Moon, "but privately…?" he trailed off with a calculating look.

"It was obviously a paid job. Somebody wanted him out of the way and hired a couple thugs to do it," said Valentine.

"That's a shame," Channyng said. He put his feet onto the desk and picked up his book, flipping through the pages idly. "Who doesn't like Dr. Simons?"

Valentine put his hands on the desk, his tall frame looming over the smaller man. "You know what, that's a good question. There's only one person I can think of."

"Who's that?" Duke asked.

Valentine and Dr. Moon glanced at him, as if noticing his presence for the first time.

"This isn't your concern," Channyng said, standing up. He grabbed Duke by the arm, steering him towards the door. "There's a lot of things I need you to do right now."

"But what about Dr. Simons?"

Valentine gave an incredulous laugh. "You really don't know, do you, Mr. Duke?"

"I don't know who killed him," he said, confused. "I'm guessing the murderer didn't leave his name and number."

Dr. Moon grunted. "Mr. Duke, he left more than that behind. He was writing a clear message to everyone, making sure we all know who's powerful and smart enough to get away with killing people who ask too many questions."

Channyng opened the door, pushing Duke out. "It doesn't concern you. I want you to help the Agriculture team today. They're down in the bay working out the kinks in their presentation."

"You want me to work with Mother? Please no," Duke said.

"Try not to make a scene. I need to talk to these gentlemen here, but I'll let you know if we learn anything."

He shut the door, leaving Duke alone in the hallway.

6

Burning Oceans

Duke got in touch with the Agriculture office, and they let him know where Dr. Tyler-Duke and her team could be found. He found the team on a quiet, deserted beach, where old nets and bits of plastic littered the sand. The sun was hiding behind dark storm clouds, while gusts of wind blew into him, sending sprays of saltwater into his face. The ocean was colorless like a black and white movie, splotched white wherever the sun shone through.

The sand leading up to the jetty was crisscrossed with tire tracks and footprints. The Agriculture team was on the jetty, and they were easy to see in their white lab coats. His mother had her graying hair in a sloppy bun, and the wind was wreaking havoc with her bangs. She was wearing clunky mud boots that looked odd paired with her brightly colored blazer and skirt. Though she wasn't the most put together person she was still the boss, strutting around with a clipboard and overseeing everyone's work.

Duke knew she saw him the moment he first stepped onto

the beach, but she kept her back towards him until he was on the jetty and came to a stop beside her.

"What do you need?" she asked, glaring at the ocean.

Duke sighed, running his fingers through his wind-blown hair. "Nothing. Channyng sent me to check on you."

"You can let him know that everything is on schedule," she said tersely, "And I don't need his PA breathing down my neck."

"Mother," he said, drawing the word out in annoyance. "I wish you'd let me help sometimes. I never wanted to do anything but work for you."

"Then you shouldn't have run off and let Channyng experiment on you."

He gave a huff of frustration. "I've told you countless times, my eyes have nothing to do with Channyng. It was some sort of anomaly that happened when I went to visit Father."

"Nothing that happened that day could have had that effect on you," she snapped. "Channyng changed your eyes, Channyng changed your temperament, and Channyng obviously changed your priorities. I certainly didn't ask you to leave Agriculture, you let him choose that for you."

They both huffed and stared aggressively at the ocean for several moments. Some of the Agriculture team were on a small motorboat, sectioning off a small portion of the bay with what looked like floating cylinders strung together as a kind of barrier. The ends were being sunk into the sand, keeping them fastened to the shore.

"Is that a floating boom, like they use for oil spills?" Duke asked, his curiosity getting the better of his irritation.

"No," his mother said, her pride in her job getting the

better of hers. "It's similar, but we crafted it specially for our new product."

"What is this new product, anyway? I keep hearing about the presentation this week, but I don't actually know what you're presenting."

"I'm sure you know that the SA is trying to get the Alliance to sponsor us in terraforming Mars," she said, and he nodded. "Well, the key to doing that - both gaining support and successfully terraforming - lies with us at Agriculture. If you had something that could both melt oceans and release oxygen into the air, don't you think you'd have a much better chance with Mars?"

"Yes," Duke said slowly, "But I think it would be impossible to do those simultaneously on that planet."

"That's where you're wrong," she said, tilting her chin. She somehow gave the impression of looking down at him even with her height of five feet and his of six. "Watch and learn." She turned towards the water where the people in the boat were signaling that they were ready. She raised a hand in acknowledgment and strode to the edge of the jetty, obediently followed by her son.

"How do you melt ice, Brandon?" she asked.

Duke watched as the boat maneuvered until it was on the outside of the barrier, bumping against it. "Heat, of course, but unless you can change the overall environment a little topical warmth isn't going to change anything."

"So we change the environment," she said passionately. "Heat can have more control on the atmosphere than you think."

"Fire can affect the atmosphere," Duke said doubtfully, "But besides that, I can't imagine what you're thinking."

She jabbed her finger into his chest. "Fire, Brandon, fire. I want to burn oceans."

"You can't burn oceans, mother."

Her eyes gleamed. "Watch me."

The boat signaled again, and Dr. Tyler-Duke raised her hand in response. Everyone on the beach stilled in expectation. All was quiet except for the dull roar of the ocean. A scientist in the boat was wearing gloves and holding a small box; after giving a dramatic nod, he threw it into the water contained by the barrier. Instantly the boat pulled away, giving the floating cylinders a wide berth.

Everyone's eyes were trained on the water. For a moment nothing happened. But then the water erupted with a brilliant orange light, adding an abrupt touch of vibrancy to the gray scene. It was like nothing Duke had seen before. It seemed identical to fire, but it rushed and spread across the surface of the water without a problem. The flames danced and skipped in a maniacal way, at one moment jumping closer to them, another moment dancing away. Every time it touched the barrier it receded back as if shocked.

Duke glanced at his mother. She was gripping her clipboard with a satisfied smirk, the reflection of the fire flickering in her eyes. Her team ran around them, calling out notes to each other and collecting data. The wind was still blowing in from the ocean, making everyone's hair stand up and tugging on Duke's unbuttoned suit. The fire was also affected. It grew closer to the jetty's edge, throwing waves of wet heat at anybody nearby.

"I'm sorry, but this will never work," Duke said, though his voice was less sure than it had been.

"This is just the first piece of the picture," his mother insisted. "And it will be enough to inspire the Alliance. If the presentation is successful, we'll be given the funds and resources we need to begin a terraforming process the world has never seen. If science can do this, there is no miracle it can't do."

"But what is it, actually? Oxygen, I assume, but you have no fuel or heat source so it's not actually fire."

She spun away on her heel with a smirk. "Come to the presentation this week. Maybe you'll learn something."

Duke pressed his lips together, hiding his clenched fists in his pockets. Before he could find a response, a ripple of concern swept over the little group. The fire had slipped past the barrier, and was making a beeline for the open ocean. The motorboat buzzed in hot pursuit.

"It's fine," Dr. Tyler-Duke said, though her son could see her unease. "They have a spray that will put the fire out immediately. We knew there was a chance the floating barrier wouldn't be high enough."

The motorboat was catching up easily. The people onboard were setting up a machine that Duke guessed held the spray. They were seconds away from a sigh of relief when the inexplicable happened.

The fire was there one moment, and gone the next. The motorboat ground to an abrupt stop and bounced back slightly, influenced by the waves. The fire had vanished in the blink of an eye. The ocean was once again gray without a trace of color as far as the eye could see.

"How is that possible?" Dr. Tyler-Duke breathed, before dashing towards the water. The boat was zipping back and forth, and even from a distance Duke could see the confusion on everyone's faces. The land crew watched, speechless.

Duke struggled down the large rocks that made up the jetty and splashed into the water to catch up with his mother. She was standing knee-deep in the ocean, her ugly boots filling with water and her bright skirt plastered to her legs. She flipped through her clipboard aggressively as if it held the answer to the phenomenon.

"Mother, you'll catch a cold," Duke remonstrated.

"It can't burn itself out. It can't. It needs the spray. Perhaps they spilled the spray into the water," she said, rattling out words a mile a minute. "This is impossible. Impossible."

"Whatever that man had in the box, I'm sure you have more of it," Duke said. "It's okay if a test burns out."

"It didn't burn out!" she shouted, whipping towards him. "It disappeared, Brandon, it's gone! I want to know why!"

"Getting yourself sick isn't going to bring it back!" he shouted back. "Get out of the water!"

"Don't pretend to care about me!"

He threw his hands into the air. "I'm sorry, Mother, I try. I try, over and over again to fix this relationship, and every time you make it seem like I'm the only one in the wrong. You want to catch your death of cold? If your work means that much to you, by all means, go ahead!"

"If only you cared about real work like you care about pandering to the president!"

"I don't pander to him, I work for him!"

"I wanted you to be a scientist!"

He turned away, running his hands through his hair furiously. "You don't understand, Mother, you never do. I'm going home."

His pants were soaked and sticking to his legs, and he could feel water squelching in his dress shoes every time he took a step. He was barely out of the water when a wave of energy hit him, causing him to stumble and grasp at his face. As he fell forward, he felt someone catch and support him, helping him sink to his knees.

All of his senses were overloaded and his fingers were tingling. Looking down, he saw faint traces of fire around his hands. Panicking, he repressed it, but the energy he felt seemed to be coming from something other than him. He fought for control of his senses, and slowly he stabilized, still on the beach with his knees on a slippery rock.

Dr. Tyler-Duke was holding his arm, staunchly bearing most of his weight. "You're as white as a sheet," she said, her eyes darting over him, searching for injuries. For a moment she was no longer a renowned scientist but just a mother. "What's wrong, son? Where does it hurt?"

"I'm fine," he stuttered. He wasn't; he could sense something in the ocean, looming behind him like a dark cloud.

"You collapsed. You're not fine," she said sharply. She cupped his face with her hand. "You're sick, aren't you? I knew you were hiding something from me. Are you dying?"

"I'm not dying," he said, pushing himself to his feet, though he was still clinging to her. "I need to get home, Mother, but keep your team out of the water. There's something wrong out there."

"I thought you weren't concerned about it."

"I changed my mind," he snapped. His eyes flickered. "Stay away from the water. I think I know what happened, but I need to talk to Channyng. If I'm right we have a huge problem on our hands."

"Fine," she relented, "We'll stay away. But I want you to get some rest. I don't know what Channyng's been making you do, but you're obviously not taking care of yourself. Go home and sleep."

Don't pretend to care about me, he thought dryly, but instead he said, "Yes, Mother. I'm sorry for yelling at you, and I'll be at the presentation. But you need to stay out of the water. Promise me."

"Promise," she said, letting him go.

7

Secrets

It was far too quiet for a world where Johnson was loose.

Jett rested his cheek on his fist. He had been staring at the sunflower pattern on the tablecloth for ages now, interrupted occasionally to sneeze due to the sheer amount of dust in Duke's house. The sun shone in a cloudy sky, pouring light into the house like milk into coffee. Tate was at the table with him, studiously reading something on a tablet he had found. Dr. Emmett was in the neighboring room, absorbed in a book, and Robbie was fast asleep on the easy-chair in his third nap of the day. Cariss was nowhere to be found.

"I'm guessing Duke's not back yet?" Parker said, coming out of the kitchen. In the drowsiness of the house she was like a breath of fresh air. Her hair was swept up in a tidy bun, and somehow she had found a way to clean and iron her clothes. Jett felt a little embarrassed when he remembered he was still wearing the wrinkled clothes he had both slept in and worn the day before.

"I haven't seen him," he answered, sitting up properly. "I wonder what he expects us to do all day. It's not like we can even take a walk without getting lost. I don't even know what country this is."

"America," Tate supplied, looking up from the tablet. "And as far as I can make out, Nova Atlantis is somewhere around where northern California used to be. I haven't yet figured out what happened to California, though."

Jett shrugged. "I don't miss it. So we're on American soil?"

"Yes and no," Tate replied. "Nova Atlantis is outside the U.S.' jurisdiction. If you live here, you have dual citizenship with Nova Atlantis and whatever country you're from. The idea was to create a fully autonomous city, giving scientists the freedom they need to further the sciences. The highest authority is the city council, which is made up of whoever the agencies vote in. The Space Agency also has a bit of say, being the most influential of the agencies."

"What do you mean, freedom to further the sciences?" Parker asked, pulling up a chair for herself.

"Apparently people began to believe that science was being hindered by social culture and morality," he explained. "A movement began with the belief that scientists should have a different eugenics code than normal people, because they serve a different purpose than normal people. For instance, their prime example was a man in 2168 who was shamed for dissecting a living pig to find a better cure for human skin cancer. It was said that that man should have been given bigger leeway. Since then the argument has been applied to everything from astronomy to chemistry."

"You learned all this on that thing?" Jett asked, gesturing at the tablet.

"This? Yeah. Duke has great internet."

Parker was frowning. "None of that is right," she said. "If science is being hindered by morality, that means whatever you call science is immoral. If this is an autonomous society, could they commit a crime to further research, and get away with it?"

"I think so," Tate said, "but I'm not sure. If it's on Nova Atlantis' soil - the city, a space station, or a space colony - then I believe they have the power to decide whether it's right or wrong."

Jett sighed, rubbing his face. "I want to get out of here and go home. I've had enough of the future. What time is it?"

Tate powered down the tablet. "Two o' clock. It feels like we've been sitting here forever."

"I managed to find the ingredients to make a chicken casserole," Parker said, trying to brighten the mood. "It's in the oven. It'll be perfect for an early supper. Do you boys like okra? I found some in the freezer that I can cook up."

"Is that the vegetable people eat in the South?" Jett asked. "I thought I heard it was sort of slimy."

Tate slumped forward, planting his face on the table. "Take me back to Nebraska!"

"Come on, boys, cheer up!" Parker scolded. She stood up, grabbing something off a nearby shelf. "Look, here's a deck of cards. Let's play crazy eights."

"We're two hundred years away from home, and the one person who can take us back is nowhere to be found. Yeah, let's just play crazy eights," Tate said sarcastically.

"Can I show you a card trick?" Jett asked, holding out his

hand. She handed him the deck and he turned it over in his hands before setting most of the cards aside. "For this trick I use twenty-one cards. Pick a card, but don't let me see it."

Parker took a card, showing it to Tate before putting it back in the downsized deck. Jett shuffled them quickly and efficiently. "Teddy taught me this. He loves card tricks."

"What are you going to tell your son Logan?" Parker asked. "Does he know Johnson's not coming back?"

Jett froze. "I almost forgot," he said weakly, before trying to pass it off with a half-hearted laugh. "Yeah, I guess I'll have to tell him."

Her face flushed. "I'm sorry. I really didn't mean to upset you. I shouldn't have asked."

"And you wonder why you're still single," Cariss said, entering the room. She had a laptop tucked under her arm and her smartphone in her hand.

Jett laid the twenty-one cards out in three piles. "Parker, is your card in pile one, two, or three?"

"Three," she said, her face burning red. "I'm sorry for asking, Jesse, and I'm sorry about Johnson. I know the past few days happened so suddenly and it's still so fresh that it's probably hard to realize it really happened, and..."

Jett was spreading the cards face-down across the table in different piles, ignoring her. "Choose two," he interrupted, and when she did he set them aside. "Two more," he encouraged, and though she opened her mouth to speak she thought better of it and said nothing. After whittling down the piles, they were left with a single card.

"Flip it over. Is that yours?" he asked.

She picked it up and gasped. "That's amazing! Tell me how you did it. You have to tell me how you did it!"

"Why would I give away my secrets?"

"Because I'm asking nicely!"

"Nice try," he smiled, gathering the cards, "but no."

"I'll figure it out. Do it again."

"I'm not about to reveal my secrets. And by the way, I'm fine."

Her lopsided smile vanished. "If there's anything I can do…"

"I'm fine," he repeated. "Though, if it's not too much trouble, I've never had okra before. I think I'm willing to try."

She jumped up eagerly. "You'll love it. I just need to find a frying pan."

He watched her disappear into the kitchen and then rubbed his face, fighting to keep his composure.

The front door squealed open and he jumped. Duke came in with a gust of wind, his hair a mess, his suit unbuttoned and his tie askew. Dark bags hung under his eyes, begging for rest. He kicked the door shut and made a beeline for Cariss.

"There's some kind of time-travel going on in the bay," he panted. His voice was raw from the cold air outside. "I felt it. I didn't notice it at first because I wasn't looking for it, but there's some kind of fluctuating rift in the water and I think Mother's project went through it!"

Cariss was by the kitchen counter, looking at her laptop, but she looked up long enough to give Duke a once-over. "You smell like seawater," she commented, as blandly as usual.

Duke ripped off his watch and pulled open a drawer, digging through it until he found a short cable. He pushed Cariss aside and used it to plug his watch into the laptop. "Look at the readings on my watch. Mother's project is in the twentieth century."

Cariss walked over to what Jett guessed was an espresso maker and turned it on. "Then follow it and see what's going on."

"You sensed time-travel?" Jett asked, hoping it was all right to join the conversation. "Could it be Johnson?"

Duke shook his head. "It didn't feel like that. His watch is more like a bubble cheating the relativity between space and time, but what I felt was more like a portal. It was like a hole in the fabric of the universe. Cariss, the power behind it was like nothing I've ever sensed before."

"If you're concerned about it, see where it goes," she said.

"You don't understand. I need help. If I find Mother's experiment on the other side, I need her equipment to take care of it. If I find Johnson then I need SA security. If I waste any time Channyng will kill me."

Dr. Emmett laid his book aside and joined them. "Why can't you let the Space Agency know that you found traces of time-travel? Surely they will understand the seriousness of the situation."

"They don't know!" Duke said, and Jett could see the fire in the man's eyes growing. "Nobody knows I'm a time-traveler but Channyng, so nobody will understand if I start talking about portals on the beach."

"I thought you said you did time-travel work for the SA," Jett said.

"Maybe I exaggerated," Duke spit back, running his hands through his hair. "The point is that as far as I know, no one has ever had the capability to time-travel besides Johnson and me. So whatever happened on the beach needs to be addressed but I don't know what to do."

"We'll go with you, Duke," Dr. Emmett said, and Jett was thankful for his grounding calmness. "Ask your mother to borrow whatever equipment you need, and then we'll take Robbie's *Starlight* to wherever your watch and senses lead us."

"I don't know what we'll find."

"I'm sure we can handle it."

Duke sighed, pressing his fists into his eyes and leaning back against the counter. "I didn't want to keep you here so long."

"We need something to do while we wait for Anton," Jett assured him. "Do you know when he'll be released from the hospital?"

"I don't," he admitted, dropping his hands. His fire waned. "Channyng wants to keep Anton around for a little bit, so I might have to bring him to Nebraska after the rest of you."

Jett's stomach dropped. "I'm not leaving without him. Your boss can't just keep him, he's my son."

"The SA has done more for him than you ever have," Cariss said bluntly.

Jett stood, dropping the cards. "Where's the hospital? I need to see him."

"Later, King," Duke said, heading towards the stairs. "I'm not sure they'd let you in without Channyng's permission, anyway."

"Then check on him for me," Jett begged. "Can't you see we're back where we started? He's trapped with people who aren't his family in a place that's not his home."

"I'm sorry, I really am. Channyng sent me reports to file, so give me a few hours in my office, then we can sort out the portal on the beach, and then I promise I'll ask about taking Anton home. But he's not my responsibility, so I'm not going back to the hospital."

"I'll go see him myself, then!"

"Go ahead!" Duke snapped, startling Jett. "I'll send someone to find you when you get lost." He stormed up the stairs.

Jett grabbed his North Face jacket and shrugged it on. A chair squeaked as Tate jumped up, snatching up his own coat. Parker left her work in the kitchen and followed them to the front door, still holding a spatula. "Don't go. You'll get lost. He's tired, Jesse, I'm sure you can tell. Give him some time to himself and he'll be in a better mood to help you."

"He's right. Anton is my responsibility, not his," Jett said, tugging on his shoes. A layer of fine red dust still clung to them, leftover from the Red Planet. "I'll take Tate with me; make sure Dr. Emmett and Robbie stay here and close. I'll try to be back in time for supper, I promise."

"I'll keep it warm," she said, giving him a tiny smile.

8

Angel's Crypt

"I'm pretty sure I saw a hospital between here and the complex," Jett said, walking up the steps that led onto the station platform. They were jostled by the late afternoon crowd. Men and women, burdened with bags, backpacks, and purses, waited in disorganized lines for the next train. Jett stopped in front of the holographic map and studied it carefully. "Where are we? Why doesn't this say where we are?"

"Hey Jett! I thought my phone was useless since it isn't compatible with the wifi or coverage here, but I just realized I can take pictures," Tate said. "Smile!" Jett gave him a blank look and he snapped a photo. "Perfect. What do you think my friends at home will think if I tell them this is my newly found father and a hologram?"

The crowd grew around them as the train grew closer. A woman with a uniformed jacket and a massive headset bumped against Jett, and he felt a brush of metal around his wrist. Alarmed, he looked down and saw the gleam of handcuffs. His police training kicked in and he twisted away before they could click shut.

Giving up her attempt at subtlety, the woman's hand shot to her side to rest on her weapon. "You're under arrest," she said quietly. She pointed with her chin to a nondescript black car, parked in the no-parking zone beside the station. "Walk to the car with your hands behind your head. No sudden movements."

Tate's eyes widened. "Wait, what did he do? We're not even from here, ma'am, we're..."

"Quiet," Jett interrupted. "Arguing isn't helpful in this kind of situation. I know from experience."

"Experience, huh? You have lots of that when it comes to cops?" the woman said.

He ignored the urge to roll his eyes. "I'm a police officer."

"Huh. Kid, you're coming too. Both of you to the car, now."

The crowd parted as she marched them off the station, and though Jett saw a few curious looks they weren't given more than a passing glance. She cuffed Jett's wrists and put him and Tate into the back seat. It was vaguely similar to the patrol car he had shared with Teddy in Nebraska, the main difference being that the floor and walls were black, and a black screen separated them from the front seats instead of bars. The woman shut the door and moments later the car started moving.

Tate felt along the window and the black screen. He grabbed the door and rattled it. "What do you think we did?" he whispered.

"Nothing," Jett said, slipping out of the handcuffs. It was a skill he and Teddy had perfected. "I know it's been two hundred years, but you'd think she'd still read us our rights. This can't be legit."

"Nova Atlantis is completely different from what we're used to," Tate pointed out. "Are we not allowed on train stations without some kind of registration?"

"I don't know."

"You dragged us out here, and you don't even know the basics of travel in this place?"

"Well, sue me for not knowing, I've never been to California!"

The car pulled into a narrow street. They were in a part of the city with less of the glass architecture and more of the old-fashioned drywall and concrete buildings. They made another turn into a narrow alley, which was empty except for a tall man in a suit, his hands in his pockets.

"This looks like the stereotypical location for a murder," Jett muttered. "If you have any good ideas of what to do, I'm all ears."

"Play dead," Tate said, sarcasm thick. "It'll be good practice for when we actually do die in a moment."

The car rolled to a smooth stop. The woman got out and opened their door.

"I'm sorry for the rude introduction," she said, and she actually sounded apologetic. "I'm Julia Valentine, and I really do work for city security, but that's not why you're here. My husband wanted to speak with you."

She was tall, and her smile reminded Jett of Maddie. Her hair was darker than Maddie's had been but was just as curly, though it was matted down by the large headset she was wearing. Her face was partly obscured by a speaking device connected to the headphones.

She held the door open as they climbed out, and she didn't

comment on the fact that Jett was holding the open handcuffs in his hand. The man in the suit swaggered over. Julia was slightly taller than them, but this man towered over them with an imposing height.

"My name is Ernest Valentine," he said. He had the voice of an orator: loud, clear, and eloquent. "I saw you with Duke yesterday, but I'm afraid I didn't catch your name."

"I'm Jett King," he said guardedly. "Why am I here?"

"I wanted to warn you," Valentine said. "You can't just wander about the city. People are looking for you."

"Why? Who?"

"Have you ever heard of Angel's Crypt?" Valentine asked, leaning against the car. "It's a popular story dating back a couple hundred years or so, popular among treasure hunters."

A couple hundred years ago, Jett had been sitting in an easychair drinking tea. "I'm not sure I know it," he said.

"Well, I'm sure you've heard of Atlantis," Valentine said. "An advanced utopia with moral people. Things went terribly wrong when the people lost that morality, and in punishment they lost their utopia."

"I've heard the story, yes," Jett said.

"I'm sure you also know that people have never stopped looking for Atlantis. Angel's Crypt is the same. A book was anonymously published with clues and riddles and a promise of unfathomable wealth."

"Isn't a crypt some kind of burial place?" Jett asked.

Valentine shrugged. "Sure, but all kinds of things can be buried."

"What does any of this have to do with us?"

"According to the preface, the Crypt will be opened by a

man known as the Sovereign," Valentine said. "As you can imagine, everyone wants to be that man. But I've always seen more in Angel's Crypt than a pile of wealth. It claims to hold a bridge between worlds, which can mean many things. I always thought it meant the secret to time-travel. But, nevermind my theories; you asked what this had to do with you. In the book, there's a riddle with an illustration of you."

Jett frowned. "I don't understand."

"Perhaps you don't, but that doesn't change the fact that you're in the book," Valentine pointed out. "I wanted to warn you about Channyng. He's obsessed with the Crypt and he'll do anything to get information out of you."

"I can assure him I don't know anything."

"But what if you do?" Valentine asked, eyeing him keenly. "I know you don't belong here. If Johnson has a time-travel watch, you could have one too. You could have hidden the treasure and written the book, for all we know."

"Sure, I'm from the twenty-first century. But I've never heard of Angel's Crypt until now," Jett said.

"This is why you kidnapped us? You think Channyng's gonna come after us over some riddles?" Tate said skeptically.

"Technically, I had every right to arrest you," Julia spoke up. "You were taking pictures. Use of cameras is prohibited in Nova Atlantis without a permit."

Tate's mouth dropped open. "I'm a juvenile delinquent!" he exclaimed. "I'm a juvenile delinquent because I was taking pictures!"

"Why are cameras prohibited?" Jett asked.

Julia shrugged. "It's more accountability than people around here want to deal with."

"But it'll make it easier for Channyng to carry you away," Valentine said. "He seems nice, but don't let his looks fool you. He's ruthless when it comes to getting what he wants, and right now he wants you two, and Anton, and anybody connected to you. He's a master of manipulation. You can't trust him, and as a result you can't trust Duke."

"I don't see why you had to kidnap us to tell us this," Jett said.

"Channyng has always believed in the Crypt, and I know for a fact he's looking for you," Valentine said. "He won't hesitate to use any means. And poor Anton is an easy target."

Jett's heart skipped a beat. "Anton's at the hospital - right?"

"Anton will never leave this city if Channyng wants him here."

"Why are you telling me this?"

Valentine smiled, ducking his head. "I confess it's selfish. Channyng's not the only one who believes that the Crypt exists."

Julia hit him in the arm. "It's true that we're interested in the legend," she said, "but we're really not trying to abduct you long-term, if you know what I mean. But if you ever do learn more about the Crypt, we'd appreciate any information you're willing to share."

"I won't guarantee I won't work against you," Valentine warned. "I want the Crypt, I won't hide that from you."

"You're obsessed with these riddles too?" Tate groaned.

Inwardly Jett echoed his groan. "Well, I appreciate your honesty, but we really don't know anything about crypts and we really don't want to get involved. And you did kidnap us. I'll call the debt paid if you give us a lift to the hospital."

"Anton's not at the hospital anymore," Valentine said, walking around the car. "Someone picked him up this morning."

"What! Who?" Jett demanded.

Julia got in the driver's seat and Valentine opened the passenger door. "I tried to tell you," the man said. "I want that Crypt, and either you or Anton are the key. Don't worry, I'll take good care of him. But I'm in this to win." He flashed one of his publicity smiles that was all teeth before getting in. The door slammed shut.

"Wait! Stop!" Jett shouted in vain. The car sped off.

9

———

Dr. Addison

In the kitchen, Duke stood bracing his hands on either side of the sink, staring down the drain. Darkness fell early this time of year, so the window was black and dull. The kitchen was dimly lit by light peeking in from the living room.

"I can't find a drying machine," he heard Parker call in frustration. "What do people use in the 23rd century, clotheslines?"

"It's the same machine as the washer," he called back moodily.

A moment later he heard Parker again. "Stop it, Robbie, you're going to break it."

"No, I know what I'm doing," Robbie said. The machine beeped in error mode, and Parker drew a long sigh.

Duke heard her soft footsteps enter the kitchen. The oven creaked open and she checked the temperature of the leftover casserole. He heard her close the oven, and then her footsteps came towards him, stopping a few feet away. "Shouldn't you look for them?" she asked softly.

He thought of a wedding. He thought of Jesse King, dead.

He thought of betrayal in Parker's eyes. "You care about them, don't you," he said, a statement rather than a question.

Parker tilted her head. "Well, yes. I consider them my friends."

He laughed bitterly. "Of course you do. Someday you'll be glad you met them, very glad. Yes, Parker Quinn, you can't see it all now but I foresee a long, happy friendship between you and the Kings!" He ended on a slightly hysterical note and hung his head. Silence reigned. Subdued, he muttered, "I'll find them, Quinn. Just give me a minute."

"Thanks," she said, weighing her words carefully. "You look like you're having a rough time, so I'll leave you alone. Get some sleep; I think you need it. But remember, I'm here if you need anything."

Her footsteps died away and Duke gave the sink a crooked smile. Water droplets clung to the faucet and around the drain, each reflecting a touch of light. It made him think of the ocean, crashing against the beach, the sun striking the waves with a million different colors. The idea of drowning felt vaguely familiar. All of the lies in his life were pooling together like drops of water, trapping him and consuming him, leaving him with no air to breathe.

Cariss' voice startled him out of his thoughts. "When are you going to take that boy home? The one who fancies himself a pilot."

Duke turned and saw her in the doorway, sipping from a mug and looking disinterested with life. "Robbie?" he said, confused.

"Robbie," she affirmed. "You know he doesn't belong here or in Nebraska. That ship isn't exactly his, either."

"Another moral dilemma, exactly what I needed." He sighed. "Robbie refuses to go home. He said he'd give up his ship if I thought he should, but he doesn't want to go back. You know he sleeps in the office in Nebraska."

"I thought you were done in Nebraska."

"I don't know! I didn't expect any of this!" Duke exclaimed, his eyes flaring. "I never meant to meet Robbie, I never meant to meet Parker, and I shouldn't have let them help me. I was excited to use time-travel for good, but I'm not sure the resulting mess was worth it."

She took a sip from her mug, an unmovable rock against his raging tempest. "Were you using time-travel for good or were you using time-travel for Channyng?"

"I know you don't like him, but it's my job. This is my life. I've been working for him since I was a nineteen-year-old kid, and he's the one who kept me from blurting out my secret for the world to know. He's not perfect, but I owe him so much."

"It doesn't take a time-traveler to know that this city isn't going to last," Cariss said. "Do you really want to be a part of it when it falls?"

"I'm not doing anything wrong."

"I'm going to assume Channyng told you that."

"We have bigger problems," Duke said. "Johnson's out there somewhere, Anton's in the hospital, there's time-travel energy in the bay, somebody killed Dr. Simons, and I'm supposed to be helping with the presentation this week alongside my Mother who hates my guts. I'm not going to rank the far off future of Nova Atlantis as top priority."

Cariss shrugged and took another sip.

Duke pushed his fingers through his hair and dragged himself away from the sink. "I'm going out. I need to find Jett."

"Be careful out there," she said. "Murder is pretty common in this city of yours. And then you should try out sleeping. You'll like it."

He nodded blearily and walked out.

Half an hour later he found them. Jett was on a bench on a deserted station, huddled in his jacket, watching the ever-twinkling lights of the city, and Tate was curled up beside him, asleep. The ocean loomed behind them.

Jett looked up at him, and Duke lowered himself on the other end of the bench, keeping Tate between them. "I'm sorry for shouting earlier," he said.

"Don't worry about it. By the way, Anton's not at the hospital. Valentine has him," Jett said, his voice muffled by his jacket.

Duke sighed. "He's one of the SA Heads, so he's probably just doing his job."

"But we're back where we started. Johnson's on the loose and my son is missing."

"I'm sorry," Duke said again.

Jett shrugged.

Duke waited a moment before gesturing at Tate. "Should we wake him up?"

Jett stretched, pushing his legs out in front of him and lifting his head. "Yeah. We were trying to get back, but we were very lost and he was tired. I'm glad you found us, it's freezing." He stifled a yawn. "I thought you said you'd send someone. You didn't have to come yourself."

"Consider this a one-time deal," Duke said. He saw a blur

of movement in the corner of his eye, and he turned to the ocean, squinting. "Is someone on the beach?"

Jett followed his gaze. "It looks like Julia Valentine," he said, surprised.

"Julia Valentine? I don't think I know her."

Jett sighed. "We met her earlier. She's some kind of cop or security guard, and she's married to Ernest Valentine."

"Huh. I've never met his family," Duke said.

The shadowy figure was walking towards them, engrossed by a tablet that lit up her face. She was holding her headset in her hand, leaving her curls free to bounce around. She lifted her head, revealing her face.

A rush of ice-cold adrenaline shot through Duke, and a flashback from ten years ago hijacked his vision, clear as day. He was finding the dead girl all over again and seeing the name *Addison* emblazoned on her shoulder. He blinked. Dr. Addison was on the beach, looking up at him.

Fast as lightning she fled. Her movements were fast and lithe like a deer, but with a certain ghost-like quality that sent shivers down his spine. He jumped off the station and into the dark, and the ground beneath his feet changed from pavement to dirt to sand.

"Where are you going?" shouted Jett.

Addison ran and the night swallowed her up. Duke stumbled and came to a stop. "Dr. Addison!" he shouted, his voice drowned out by the pounding of the ocean. "Dr. Addison, come back!"

Jett caught up to him. "That's Julia Valentine, I told you!"

"Her name is Dr. Addison," panted Duke, "and she died ten years ago, same day as my father."

Jett frowned. "You must be mistaken."

"I found her! I saw her dead!" he shouted. He shoved his shaking hands through his hair and his eyes burned. "I was on the station. I was inside and I saw her dead."

"What's going on?" Tate called groggily. He was on the platform, his silhouette black against the light of the station.

"Let's go back to your house, Duke," Jett begged. "It's dark and cold and wet out here. We'll find her, okay? If she's married to Valentine she'll be easy to find again."

"I'm sorry, I'm sorry," he babbled. He felt the first drop of rain on the back of his neck and he shivered.

They stumbled toward the light of the station, though Duke shot a final glance over his shoulder. There was nothing behind him but the wet sand and the black void of the ocean.

10

Into the Storm

The next morning, there was a watery sun in the sky and a hint of dew in the air as Duke walked across the docking bay. Cariss was beside him, and he could physically feel the weight of her eyes silently judging him for searching the internet for answers all night (in vain) instead of sleeping. Robbie, walking on his other side, looked mildly concerned.

Dr. Emmett was behind them, thoughtfully taking in how the metal walkway reflected the weak light, and watching seagulls circle overhead. Parker Quinn, quieter than usual, Jett, and Tate completed the group.

The dock was far busier than it had been before, like an anthill that had been stirred up. There were maintenance teams dressed in gray coveralls with the SA insignia on their shoulders, drinking from cans and swapping stories. There was an inspector in a sharp suit lecturing a man who seemed bored. There was a group of casual dressers on some kind of tour.

As always, quite a few people recognized Duke, pointing

and nudging their friends and coworkers. Curious glances were cast at the strangers accompanying him. Duke gritted his teeth; the staring was bad enough, but to make his morning worse, he was in the middle of a call with his mother.

"I don't see why you need my equipment," her voice said through his watch. "If you know where the fire is, tell me, and I'll get my team on the spot! I don't want you running around with my things without good reason."

"Mother, don't make me call Channyng and have him make it an order," he said, getting desperate.

She gasped. "If I hadn't already disinherited you, that's what I'd be doing right now. You're trying to coerce your own mother into giving you a top-secret product I've spent most of my life developing! How dare you!"

His brain scrabbled for a way to avoid his mother's wrath. They reached a line of tall, metal gates, and he sought out one and popped open the cover of a keypad where a latch or handle would reasonably be. He typed in a passcode and the gate began to creak open. On the other side, the *Starlight* glinted like a beacon.

Duke felt a hand on his arm. "Isn't that Anton?" Robbie whispered. Duke followed his gaze. A few gates down, Valentine was typing in a passcode. A small figure stood beside him, clutching a backpack. His hair was shorter in the back, making him look like Tate from behind, but a mop of curls was just barely visible atop his head.

Duke stared, momentarily frozen. His brain was a house where the power had been abruptly cut. *I'm hallucinating,* he thought. *This is what happens when you don't sleep for five days.*

His mother was still yapping on his watch and Valentine's gate was sliding open when a ruckus started.

A bulky car with the emblem of Nova Atlantis Security barrelled down the walkway, despite it being meant for pedestrians. Workmen, inspectors and casually dressed people screamed and jumped out of the way. The walkway was raised off the ground several feet to give better access to ships; several people vaulted over the edge, barely in time.

"Duke, what's happening?" Parker cried.

Duke's mind short-circuited. *Who is Security after?* He thought. Aloud, he apologized to his mom and hung up on his call. Valentine abandoned his gate and headed toward him, and Duke frowned in suspicion. He shoved Robbie through their gate. "Start the ship. Cariss, get everyone inside."

"Duke, my old friend!" Valentine called. The bulky car pushed closer. Valentine caught up to them, smiling his usual shark-grin. "Take Anton," he said, "Take him wherever you're going, or to Nebraska, I don't care. I'll explain later."

"Why are the cops here?" Jett asked.

Valentine's mask dropped, leaving him looking almost as tired as Duke felt. "Channyng's after the kid," he said. "I need you to get him out of here, King."

Duke pushed between them. "We're not taking him. He's supposed to be in Channyng's custody."

"Oh for goodness' sake!" Parker exclaimed. "Let's take Anton and go!"

The bulky car barreled closer. "Dr. Emmett, get Parker and Tate into the *Starlight*," Duke snapped. The doctor glanced towards the walkway and then quickly did what he was told.

That left four of them behind - a strange square with tense, intersecting lines. Anton and Jett were eyeing each other with similar faces of apprehension; Valentine had resumed his wolfish grin and was looking at Duke. "So, Brandon Tyler-Duke, what's it going to be?"

"I'm going to call Channyng," he said, his eyes burning steadily. "He told me he'd take care of Anton."

"Have you ever stopped to wonder what taking care of him means?" Jett demanded.

"Since when were you on Valentine's side?" Duke fired back. "I'm not helping him break the law! He's playing us to get what he wants. Channyng has nothing but Anton's best interests in mind."

The car swerved up to the gates, and a hail of bullets went over their heads, ricocheting in every direction. "Is that in his best interest?" Jett yelled. He ducked behind the open gate and dragged Anton with him.

Duke and Valentine scrambled inside. There was a keypad on this side of the gate as well; Valentine punched in the code and it began to slide shut.

"Come out from there with your hands behind your head!" a voice shouted over a megaphone. "We don't want to harm you, but we will use any force necessary to secure the boy."

"I do not know what is happening. I did not do anyzing," Anton said, bewildered.

Another round of bullets hit the gate. "Whatever happened to the laser pistols everyone had on Reka?" Jett grimaced, eyeing the gate's slow progress.

"Believe it or not, they use these because they're more

intimidating," Valentine grinned. "And intimidation and bullying is the entire job description of Security."

"Are you telling me this is a normal occurrence?"

Valentine peeked through the closing gap and jumped back as another round began. "More or less. This city's a mess."

The gate ground shut. The *Starlight* hummed in the background. Jett grabbed Anton's arm, who followed him like a rag doll, and dashed toward the ship. Duke got in his way and all three of them stumbled. "King, I'm serious, this needs to stop," Duke said, his voice panicked. "Something's wrong and we're not going to make it better by resisting. Let me talk to Channyng and I swear things will be okay!"

"They're forcing the gate open," Valentine said, pushing against the metal. "For once in your life, Duke, listen to someone besides Channyng and get out of here, now!"

"No! If they're after you I'm guessing they have a reason!"

The gate was swinging open. The useless barrage against the metal wall was still going, and the shots were growing louder. Valentine pushed his shoulder against the gate, grimacing at the weight. "Channyng wants Anton," he said. "He told me not to take him from the hospital but I did anyway. That's the story, thanks for making me share it while we're being shot at!"

"So we're in the wrong," Duke reasoned. He pointed at the slowly opening gate. "They're in the right, not us! Hello! Hello! I'm Duke, the SA president's assistant! Let me talk to Channyng!"

Jett dragged Anton to the *Starlight.* The gate kept opening.

"Send out the boy!" the voice outside blared. "This is your last chance to abide by the law!"

"Look, Duke, I'll meet you on Rendova," Valentine said desperately. "That's where you're going, huh? I'll find you and I'll explain."

"Rendova?" Duke repeated. "How did you know that?"

"You're following the portal in the bay, right? The timestream isn't steady, so be careful of what day you end up there. I'll buy you some time. Get out of here!"

Duke's brain stopped again. Valentine turned toward the sound of bullets and straightened his tie before marching out of the opening gate, grinning a smile that was all teeth.

Duke hesitated, but the word *Rendova* propelled him into the *Starlight*. He shut the door with finality.

Robbie was behind the controls. "They're through the gate," he muttered, flicking on the viewing screens. A steady *pinging* began against the side of the ship and his eyes narrowed. "What? They're shooting the *Starlight*? First of all, highly ineffective. Second of all, how dare they!"

"Get us out of here!" Jett demanded.

"Where are we going, Duke?" Robbie asked, his fingers flying over the control panels.

"I put in the space and time coordinates you had on your watch," Cariss said. "Does Rendova Island, 18th century sound right?"

"Yes, that's right," Duke said, claiming the seat between Robbie and Cariss. "I haven't run any calculations yet, so I don't actually know what kind of conditions we'll be flying into…"

"We'll calculate when we get there!" Robbie said, flipping a lever. "Sit down, everybody. We're about to run entirely on the time-key and the field displacer, so this ride will be anything but smooth."

Jett pushed a trembling Anton into one of the backseats where the others were ready and waiting. He was just sitting down himself when everyone was flung from their chairs.

"Robbie!" Parker screamed.

"Artificial gravity! Turn it on!" Cariss shouted.

The ship spasmed and rolled, and the viewing screens cut out. One moment Duke was in mid-air, and the next he was crashing against the ceiling.

"It failed! The *Starlight* is dead!" Robbie yelled from somewhere. The inside of the ship was pitch black but it was clear that they were rolling. Something shattered and Tate yelled. Duke was rolled across the floor and then onto the wall, and then he was thrown through a spray of shattered glass. He reached for a lever before being pulled and flung away from it.

"Cariss, we can't stop it!" he panicked. He slammed against the control panel. "Cariss! Cariss?"

"Duke, what's..." Dr. Emmett began, but his voice cut off with a sharp cry.

The ship spasmed again, and all eight of them were flung across the small space and into the wall. With a shudder the ship went still. Duke tried to lift his head, but it was spinning too much and felt too heavy. He dropped his forehead against the floor and as he hovered on the edge of consciousness, the only thing he could hear was Tate crying.

11

A Team Divided

Jett lifted his head and groaned. He pushed himself up and pain seared across his head. He managed to sit up and slump against the wall. Nearby, Duke was fumbling with his watch, and Robbie was clutching his arm.

"I'm so sorry," the pilot whimpered. "I should have let you run the calculations, Duke. I'm so sorry."

"You couldn't have known," Duke said, propping himself against the wall. He had a gash across his face, but his healing speed was extraordinary, so Jett guessed it wouldn't be there for long.

"What happened?" Jett asked.

"That's what I'm trying to figure out," Duke said, lifting up his watch.

It would have been total darkness without the light from Duke's watch. The ship was tilted slightly, making the wall behind them lower than the opposite one. One of the main viewing screens was shattered, and the four chairs up front were missing various pieces - armrests, backs, and cushions. The door had been dislocated. The lower half had been driven into the floor, causing a gap between the upper half and the doorframe. It was dark outside, but Jett heard the harsh pounding of rain and saw a trickle of water on the inside of the door.

All eight of them were in a line against the wall: Parker, Dr. Emmett, Jett, Tate, Robbie, Anton, Duke and Cariss. It was the first time the eight of them had been together since that day at the Communications Center on Reka where they had first met Anton. *What a reunion*, Jett thought miserably. He heard his uncle moving beside him, and he felt a careful touch on his arm.

"Are you all right?" Dr. Emmett asked.

"I think so," he answered. "A little banged and bruised, but I don't think anything's broken. What about you?"

"Same." The older man sat up with a grunt. "Where are we? Is this Earth?"

"This is Earth, yes," Duke said, standing up. He wobbled precariously on the tilted floor. "We're on Rendova Island. According to my watch, there's a tropical storm outside. The *Starlight* wasn't expecting it. I think we hit some trees straight away that knocked out the power."

He started messing with the control panel, and Robbie shook his head. "It's not gonna work. The *Starlight's* in pieces, Duke."

"I'll take care of it. Doctor, could you look at his arm?" he said.

Emmett shuffled over, pulling a flashlight out of his pocket and investigating Robbie's arm. "Your shoulder is dislocated. I'm going to pop it back in," he said gently. "Hold still for me."

Jett fought back nausea as he heard the doctor push it into place and Robbie's sharp intake.

Duke was prying up a piece of the control panel. "What are you doing?" Jett asked.

"The ship is dead, but I can still use the time-key and the field displacer," Duke explained grimly. "I'm going to send us right back to where we came from, and then I'm taking every one of you to Channyng like he asked me to."

"No!" Jett exclaimed. "What are you thinking?"

"I'm thinking I don't want all of you to die because you don't trust me!" Duke snapped. "Look at us, King. If you had let me do my job we wouldn't have wrecked the *Starlight*. We're going back."

"Let him do it, Jesse," Dr. Emmett said. "We'll just have to deal with the consequences."

"Look, Valentine warned me about this," Jett said.

Duke's eyes flared. "Valentine is married to a dead woman. Valentine breaks the law for fun. Valentine throws his rank into my face every chance he gets. Don't talk to me about Valentine!"

"Calm down," Dr. Emmett said.

Duke turned his back to them and continued to disassemble the panel.

Cariss sat up, pushing shards of glass out of her hair. "This is where the portal leads?" she asked skeptically, watching the rain trickle over the door.

Duke lifted his wrist, showing off his watch. "I was a day off," he seethed, "a day off! The portal leads to a wet but calm

Tuesday, and that's when Mother's fire will appear. And I got us here on a *Monday*, during an honest-to-goodness cyclone!"

"I should have let you double check," Robbie said, still clutching his arm.

Duke pushed his fingers through his hair. "You should have let me talk to Channyng!"

"Calm down!" Dr. Emmett ordered. "Duke, stay focused. Robbie, no one's blaming you."

"This ship is going to be flooded if we don't do something," Cariss said, standing up with a hand on the wall for balance.

"I checked the details on my watch. The rain will stop for the night. Unless I'm a day off again," Duke said bitterly.

"We must have hit the tail end of the storm, then," Cariss surmised. "That's still a lot of water on the floor, though."

"The ship's in pieces, and she's worried about water damage," Robbie said, slightly hysterical.

She stuffed several pieces of the pilot seats into the gap to slow the trickling water. Dr. Emmett was kneeling next to Parker, trying to wake her up, and Jett realized he should probably check on the twins. They were on the other side of Robbie, lying side by side.

Tate's face was slack, and blood dripped from his hair onto the floor. Anton was conscious and was the closest to the door, so his clothes were soaked with rainwater. He was shivering, but he stilled when Jett knelt beside him.

"You okay?" Jett asked softly.

"Yes, sir," he answered, barely above a whisper. "I do not

understand what happened. I tried to stay in ze hospital, but ze man insisted."

"It's not your fault," Jett assured him. "Are you injured anywhere?"

"I do not zink so." With great effort he sat up. One of his arms was wrapped in gauze while the other looked raw and scarred, and Jett remembered that he had been in the hospital for burns. Besides that, he looked relatively unharmed.

Jett gazed at him for several moments, at a loss of what to say. Ever since he'd made the decision to find his son, he'd run into one setback after another. Now that they were face to face he didn't have a clue of what to do next. The boy was hunched forward slightly, his arms folded tightly across his chest.

"You look like your mother," Jett blurted, and then mentally berated himself, thinking *what on earth was that?*

The boy looked at him guardedly. "Zat is what Mr. Johnson says. Zough he says I have similarities to bof of my parents."

Inwardly Jett gave a sigh of relief, thankful that Anton was willing to talk. "You look mostly like Maddie, I think. Tate looks more like me."

Anton paused. "I zink zat is impossible, sir. I do not understand it very well, but I zought zat we are ze exact same person, wight? Nobody has explained it all to me yet so I am sorry if I am wrong. But I zought Duke and Mr. Johnson said zat one of us was a copy because of a paradox. One is extra, I zink?"

"Well, maybe," Jett admitted. "But I don't know. You both seem very different, and very real, if you know what I mean."

A loud *thud* interrupted them. Duke had thrown his weight against the door, to little effect. He stepped back and hit it again, shoulder first. This time there was creaking and scraping of metal as the door budged slightly.

"What are you doing?" Dr. Emmett asked.

"I need to see the outside of the ship," he answered. His eyes were more subdued than they had been; now they were tired, flickering coals. "I need to look at the damage to make sure I'm not leaving half of it behind."

He threw himself against it once more and it broke free. He barely caught himself as it tried to dump him out, falling forward like a gang-plank. The pounding of the rain rose to be deafening, and water splattered over him, wetting his hair and rolling down his starched suit.

"We're going to get soaked," Dr. Emmett shouted over the roar of the storm.

"The wind is blowing away from the door," Duke shouted back. "That should help keep the water out."

He stepped out and Jett saw him stagger against the force of the wind before stumbling out of sight. Cariss took over the work of dismantling the panels, and Dr. Emmett moved over to Tate to evaluate his injuries. Parker was sitting up now, pushing her hair out of her face and gazing in awe at the torrential downpour.

Outside were the dim outlines of trees that made up the grove that the *Starlight* had crashed into. Any visibility was considerably dampened by the rain. The reality of the situation dawned on Jett, and his heart skipped a beat. Rendova Island was worlds away from what he was used to in Nebraska. He was a fool to think he could keep himself and Anton there until Valentine arrived. For a moment he entertained the idea of simply letting Duke return them to Nova Atlantis, but he quickly dismissed it. The memory of gunfire was enough to bring him back to his senses.

If he had to pit himself against Duke to save his son, then so be it.

12

The Right Thing

Water cascaded off Duke's hair and over his face and more water trickled down his collar. With the state of his jacket, he was internally drafting a letter to his tailor, renouncing him and his 'water-resistant' lies. The large hatch door on the back of the *Starlight* that housed the pod was unaligned with the doorframe, so to keep it from falling off he had scrounged up some emergency straps and was trying to tie it shut.

With the rain pounding around him, he didn't notice that Dr. Emmett had come out until he stepped directly into his line of sight. "Need help?" the doctor asked, voice raised to be heard.

Duke shook his head, flinging water left and right. Despite his rejection, the doctor stayed, silently watching him work. Duke tugged on one of the straps, straining to pull it tight, but it slipped off of the hump of the ship and dropped into a pile in front of him.

He stared at it for a moment, stunned that things could get any worse. Scrubbing his face with his hands, he turned and slumped against the *Starlight*, sitting in a puddle of water.

"I'm sorry," he said, rubbing his eyes with his fists. He knew he must look like a child. "I didn't mean to lose my temper. I'm exhausted. I shouldn't have yelled at Jett, and goodness, I yelled at Robbie. He didn't even do anything."

"I wish I could put more stock in your apologies, Duke," Dr. Emmett said, not unkindly. "But you have a habit of turning around and repeating the same offense, no matter how sincere your regret was."

"I know, I know," he groaned. "But I try, don't I? To do the right thing."

Dr. Emmett sank to a crouch, putting them back at eye-level. "Do you?"

Duke's eyes snapped up. "You don't see what I go through every day. Everyone at work is always trying to provoke me; they think it's funny to get me riled up so they can see my eyes. And my mother thinks she's so much better than me because she's actually a scientist and not an *assistant*. Like she doesn't have three assistants. I mess up sometimes, but I think I deserve a little grace at this point."

Dr. Emmett shook his head. "Duke, I used to think your ability to time-travel was what made you different. It's the usual excuse for your behavior. But now that I've seen the kind of people you work for and the environment you surround yourself with, I believe I understand you better."

"What... what do you mean?"

"You're just a normal person in Nova Atlantis. They made that city to give them power without limits and science without ethics. You think your time-traveling capabilities put you outside of the rules, just like what they tried to do with Nova

Atlantis. But right and wrong are always the same, no matter who or where you are."

"Don't I deserve a little breathing room?" Duke cried. "I'm not like you or Jett. I'm not a nobody from Nebraska. My life is so much bigger, and louder, and everything I do is so much more stressful because the pressure is always on and everything I do is actually consequential. I can't catch a break, Emmett. The first time I yelled at my mother was put on international TV, for goodness' sake."

"You can't say your life is any more consequential than Jett's."

"Look at the man!" Duke laughed bitterly. "He managed to lose a baby - how do you even do that? - and nobody gave him flak for it. No, we cheered and slapped him on the back for leaving his precious easy-chair to find the son we conveniently found for him and he gets rewarded by getting to go back to his normal, perfect life!"

"I believe Jett's biggest flaw is inaction," Dr. Emmett said seriously. "Instead of the right thing or the wrong thing, he chooses nothing. But he's trying his best to change, and we both have seen it, so don't scorn him. And as a time-traveler, you should know better than anybody that it's often the seemingly inconsequential people that make the best differ-ence in the world."

Duke sighed, running his fingers through his hair. Rain trickled down his hands and wrists. "I want to do the right thing, but people keep changing their minds about what the right thing is."

"Right and wrong never change."

"Then you'd think people would finally have them figured out by now."

"Duke, I know you. You know these things. If the people around you don't, I really think you're wasting your life in Nova Atlantis."

"I'm afraid I wouldn't know what to do if I were to leave it," Duke said.

Dr. Emmett shrugged. "Then stay and change it. From what I've seen, Nova Atlantis was made so that the smart and powerful people could decide what is right and wrong. Jett should let you lose your temper and trample over his input, because he's a nobody and you're a genius. Is that really what you believe?"

"No," he said, barely audible over the rain. "The standard is the same. Right and wrong don't change."

"So you need to be held accountable, just like Jett, just like anybody."

"Most of my mistakes happen because I was just following orders, though," he protested feebly.

"Does that really change anything?"

He shook his head, defeated. "No."

Dr. Emmett squeezed his shoulder, standing up. "You aren't any more entitled than anybody else. The people you work for aren't, either. If they do something wrong it's wrong, no matter what they say."

Duke thumped his head against the *Starlight*, tipping his face towards the sky. He closed his eyes against the beating of the rain. "I'm tired, Dr. Emmett. I'm so tired."

"Let's step inside for a bit, Duke," he said gently. "You're not in this alone. If Nova Atlantis has really led you to believe that right and wrong depend on the person, that's a terrible, heavy weight to carry. You can put it down. That's too much for any man."

"I can't go back in. I don't know what to do."

"You don't have to," Dr. Emmett pointed out. "Let the rest of us help. That's what friends are for."

He put his hand on Duke's shoulder, guiding him into the ship. Duke nearly slipped as he stepped onto the tilted floor with his wet shoes, but he caught himself on the doorframe. Cariss was continuing the work on the panels, while Robbie and Jett were still on the floor with the twins. Parker was waiting by the door.

"So, what's the plan?" she asked, looking from Duke to Jett.

Duke spoke first, out of habit. "I have a bit of work left to do, but I'm fairly certain I can get the *Starlight* back to the Nova Atlantis dock."

"I say we wait here for Valentine," Jett said.

"The man's a liar," Duke said wearily. "He knew about the portal which means he is either a time-traveler himself or he knows one. He never told anyone."

"Sounds familiar," Cariss said dryly, giving him a pointed look.

"My powers are a Space Agency secret. There's even a file somewhere. But I'm pretty sure that Valentine is just another Johnson," Duke said.

"We'll vote on it," Parker interrupted, and Duke almost laughed. It was just like her to come up with a solution that was as diplomatic as it was childish. "We can go back to Nova

Atlantis right away, or we can wait here until tomorrow to talk with Valentine. I vote we wait."

"I think we should go back, obviously," Duke said.

"I vote we stay," said Jett.

"There's no reason to stay," Cariss said. "As much as I dislike Channyng, we have to go back eventually, so why put it off?"

"I have to agree," Dr. Emmett said. "Tate needs a hospital. We need to consider the basics of survival, like food and water. We don't have any of that here."

"I can make it," Tate said, though his voice was slurred. "I think we can stay here until Valentine comes. We need answers, don't we?"

Duke looked at Robbie. "What about you?"

Robbie gave a one-shouldered shrug. "I'm gonna agree with whatever you say, man. If you think we should go back, then we'll go back."

"Anton?" Dr. Emmett prompted.

The boy shrank into himself. "I do not know. I suppose I zink we should stay here."

"Good job, Parker, four against four," Tate said sarcastically. "This was a great idea. You really thought this through."

"Guys, there are eight of us here," Parker said, arguing her position. "I think the eight of us, working together, can last twenty-four hours. I mean, really! Think about what we've done already."

Robbie shook his head. "I'm useless without my ship."

"Your ship is still helping us," she pointed out. "It's providing shelter."

"Then fine, I guess, use it as a hotel if that's the only thing it's good for. All it needs is bagels and orange juice."

Duke glanced at Dr. Emmett before approaching Jett, crouching beside him. "King," he said quietly, "If you'd like to stay here, I'll stay here. But on one condition."

"What?"

"You call the shots," he said, "and I get to sleep for once. Deal?" He offered his hand.

Jett hesitated, but only for a moment. "Deal," he said, shaking it.

13

Johnson, Channyng, Valentine

Channyng was a man of average height and build, with almond eyes, defined cheekbones, and raven-black, straight hair. He was very well put together in a very modern sort of way. His hair and nails were perfectly cut and manicured, his loafers were made from crocodile leather, and his suit was well tailored and his dress pants were stylishly tight. Though he looked Asian, his family had actually immigrated to the U.S. generations ago and had since become wealthy and influential.

But despite his chill, rich-boy persona, Teddy Johnson knew him as the most ruthless man he had ever met.

Johnson knocked on the president's door. "Come in," he heard, and he pushed it open. Channyng was slouched in his chair, his feet propped up on his desk, looking at his tablet. He raised his brows when he saw Johnson, and then waved at a chair nonchalantly. "Take a seat. I wasn't expecting you to show up here."

"Where else would I be?" Johnson asked, taking the chair. "I'm a man in need. We've only met briefly in the past, but I've heard that you're more lenient on people in trouble than anyone else in this city, and I'll do anything you want to get what I want."

"Well, I do own this city," Channyng said, setting his tablet aside. "Not only is the SA the most prominent Agency here by far, but I'm on the city council. So, if you want something, there ain't no better place to get it than right here. Can't say I'll give it to you, but out of curiosity, what do you want?"

Johnson clenched his fists. "I want Anton."

Channyng shrugged, picking a book up off the desk and flipping through it. "I know, buddy. I never told Valentine he could take him; anybody knows that. I sent Security after them, so no worries. You're kinda attached to the boy, huh?"

"He's mine," Johnson asserted. "And you'd better watch yourself. I know you're interested in him."

"I'm interested in a lot of things," Channyng said mildly. "When I asked what you wanted, I really thought you'd ask for something bigger, man."

Johnson sighed. "You know what else I want. I want to stay out of jail, and I want my colony back."

"The SA's colony, if you don't mind. Don't forget who put you there," Channyng said. "Ivan's money, along with my vote and influence… you owe us a lot, don't you? Especially since you never told me you could time-travel."

"You owe me just as much!" Johnson argued. "I fought for and started that colony long before you were born."

"Then you time-traveled away," Channyng reminded him, "and who took care of it while you were gone, and sent people to live there to take care of it? Yours truly. You were just a tenant, buddy. I'm the landowner."

"You little blackguard! You said the colony was mine to own."

"And look how that ended," he said flatly. "You gotta understand the position I'm in, Mr. Johnson. Everybody knows I liked you and that I voted for you as president of Reka, but now that people know what you've done, it would look bad if I supported you. I voted for you because I thought you'd make the SA look good, and instead you caused a famine, started riots, set up an illegal force field, and then got arrested because of said force field."

"Enough," Johnson growled. "Look here, are you willing to help me, or am I wasting my time?"

Channyng pulled his feet off the desk, tossing his book aside. "I could get you Reka, but I don't think it's the right decision. Everyone has already marked it off as a failure, so why go back? Nobody will go with you, and ruling a kingdom with no subjects isn't fun. I can get you a cozy office job here at the complex."

"Are you insane? I don't want a cozy office job! Thanks to your wretched assistant, everyone in the world knows me as a time-traveler and a crook."

"No need to get worked up. You must know, I didn't realize it was you time-traveling when I sent Duke after you, so you gotta forgive me. No office job then. Honestly man, I think the smartest thing for you at this point would be to get your watch back and leave for good."

"I want my colony!" Johnson seethed. "You don't know what I've been through. I survived injuries and the terrors of Reka I to shut off the force field. I was on short rations for months, and I often gave away what little food I had to Anton since I couldn't bear to see him hungry. I watched my men grow gaunt and wither away."

"Monologue. I almost forgot you did that," Channyng nodded, wholeheartedly disinterested.

"The suffering I endured for that colony is something you could never understand," Johnson continued. "Every night, I watched the stars. There are millions out there, far more than you could ever see on Earth. 'If I'm so enraptured with them now,' I would think, 'when my people are dying and my dream is fading, how much brighter will they shine when I have returned Reka to its former glory?'"

"Dude," Channyng said, "I'm not giving you Reka. We're shutting that program down. I mean, a frozen wasteland and a Red Planet that eats people? I think there's something in the water that's been messing with your heads. It's time you all moved out."

"Then I want my name cleared, and Anton Venedict returned to me," Johnson said. "And a paid trip to North Asia, and a cabin."

"That's where the boy's people are from, right?" Channyng asked, studying his nails.

Johnson hesitated. "Yes. Anton was born on Reka, but his parents were refugees."

Channyng smiled, shaking his head. "Liar," he said. "Anton's father is named Jett King, who is a very boring man from Nebraska. I don't care if you kidnap children and make them live through famines, but don't ever lie to me again."

"Did Duke tell you?" Johnson fumed. "You need to keep that man out of my business! I would have never been arrested if you hadn't sent him looking for time-travel!"

Channyng held up his hands. "I'll keep him out of your business from now on."

The intercom buzzed, and Channyng sighed. "Who is it?"

"Officer Bryant, sir," a clipped voice answered. "We have Valentine in custody, sir. He was attempting to escape with Anton Venedict, sir, and he distracted us long enough that the boy managed to get away. Sir."

"Tell your supervisor to drop your pay for your failure, but to give you a raise for your commendable respect toward your superiors," Channyng said, swiveling his chair back and forth. "And do you have Valentine? Send him in and keep looking for Anton."

"Yes sir," the officer said. "But I think he'll be difficult to find, sir. There was an unregistered spacecraft in the dock, named the *Starlight*, and it simply disappeared. We can't find a trace of it, sir. Sir."

Channyng paused for a moment. "Keep an eye out anyway," he shrugged. "And really, officer, I love your manners. I've got more ranks and titles than you have friends, so it's nice to be appreciated. You're dismissed." He ended the call and glanced across the desk at Johnson. "Security officers. They're hilarious."

The door swung open and the officers pushed Valentine in, slamming it shut behind him. Johnson wasn't sure if he had seen this man before. He had spent quite a bit of time with the SA when he was campaigning to be Reka's president, but the members were continually changing and it had been several years back.

Valentine straightened and smoothed out his ugly tie, and then gave them a smile that looked more like a dog baring its teeth than anything. "Any kombucha, Channyng? You know how I love that stuff. You usually have some around here."

"I could take away everything you have," Channyng said bluntly. "You know I'd hate to do that, but what's a president to do?"

"There's nothing you could do to me that I couldn't handle," Valentine said, tilting his chin arrogantly.

Channyng sighed, brushing lint off of his jacket. "Your wife Julia is a sweet woman. Remember how we worked so hard to give her a new identity, because of all that secret agent business she used to do? It'd be a shame if people learned she never really died."

Valentine opened his mouth soundlessly for a moment, and then snapped it shut. He shoved his hands into his pockets. "What do you want?"

"I just want to know why you went against my orders and took Anton from the hospital. And where you put him."

Valentine rolled his eyes. "You know I'm just as interested in Angel's Crypt as you are. I've got to stay a step ahead of you."

Johnson frowned. "What's Angel's Crypt?"

"What's he doing here?" Valentine asked with a jump of surprise. "I thought he was on the run, trying to stay out of the slammer."

"He's not going to the slammer. You're going to side with

me and vote to let him go, free of any charges," Channyng said calmly.

"That's ridiculous."

"Think of how much I've done for you, Ernest. You and your wife would have never gotten a life together if I hadn't stepped in and helped you after the station exploded. I kept your little secret for ten years."

"No wonder you're so nice," Valentine said, looking him in the eye. "Kindness is the best bribery there is. Better watch out, Johnson, he's handing you freedom on the end of a chain."

"Now that that's settled," Channyng continued, "I want to know where Anton is."

Valentine barked a sudden laugh. "I'll tell you where Anton is," he said. "He's in Duke's ugly ship, getting far away from here and never coming back."

Channyng's brow quirked up, and Johnson jumped from his chair with all the rage of a mad bull. "He's *what?* You kidnapped him and gave him to *Duke?* Since when did Anton belong to *you?* You'd better hope you're wrong! Anton has no business with Duke, or Jett, or any of those scoundrels!"

"Sit down," Channyng said, not even sparing him a glance. "Ernest, I find it very hard to believe that my personal assistant would run away like that."

"Maybe he's done with you," Valentine leered. "You never let him reach his full potential. You kept him strapped to you like a dog on a leash."

"That's what he is," Channyng said calmly, "And he knows

it as well as anyone. A dog is a very good example, Ernest. They always return to their owner."

"Well, he's not coming back with Anton."

"Wait and see. I predict he'll be back not only with Anton, but Jett and the rest of them. He'll march them up to my front door and ask what I'd like him to do next."

A look of uncertainty flickered in Valentine's eyes as he waged an internal battle, trying to believe in Duke's goodness rather than Duke's complicity. At length, the truth won out. "Perhaps you're right," he relented. "And perhaps you do get Anton back. But I've got Jett King on my side, and we both know he's the real key to finding Angel's Crypt."

"Again, what is Angel's Crypt?" Johnson demanded.

Channyng groaned. "Just what we need, Ernest, more competition. Goodness, you're kinda dense sometimes."

Valentine shrugged and dug his hands deeper into his pockets. "I'm going home. Time will tell if Duke is truly loyal to you, or is willing to side with people who are more honorable than any of us put together. And Channyng, you'd better keep Johnson quiet. If he says a word about Julia I'll kill him second and you first."

Channyng shrugged, propping his feet back onto the desk. "No worries, no worries. And you'll see; Duke wouldn't know what to do without me."

Valentine strode out of the room, swaggering as if he hadn't just been cowed into submission by a smaller man in skinny dress pants. Johnson frowned, turning back to the desk. "What's the big deal about his wife?"

"Do you really think I'd tell you?" Channyng said. "So, tell me, where have you been all of this time? Did you crash the

Kenswick? If you did, I'm impressed, but I'm also kinda angry since that ship cost a lot and some of the people who died voted for me."

"No, I didn't crash it," Johnson growled. "And no, I'm not telling you where I've been. The only reason I came to you at all is because I want Reka, I want Anton, and I want Security off my tail. If you can't help me I'm out of here."

Channyng made a clicking sound with his tongue. "If I can't help you, it's game over for you. You'll be locked away and they'll throw away the key. What makes you think I'll help you, anyway? I used to like you, but that was before you made a mess of Reka."

"Anybody knows you love putting people in your debt," Johnson pointed out. "All I want is my name cleared. You can do that, you can do anything. You killed Dr. Simons the other day and nobody cared."

"You're right, nobody cared." Channyng laughed softly. "Nobody cares enough to look for evidence, and of course, since this is Nova Atlantis there were no security cameras. You know, that's what I like about this place."

"What, no cameras?"

Channyng smiled, shaking his head. "No. I like that nobody cares."

14

Rendova

The *Starlight* was in a grove of trees, half-buried in the sandy ground. There were several thin trees that had been snapped in half by the ship's crash, and branches and gigantic leaves covered the ground, along with the occasional coconut. The morning sun was weak and hidden by rain clouds. There were several inches of standing water around the *Starlight*, and the rain was steadily increasing it.

Jett inhaled deeply, tasting damp air. Between the rain and the flooding he was soaked to the bone. He had left his North Face jacket inside the ship, and it was reassuring to have even one piece of dry clothing to look forward to. He stood behind the *Starlight*, tying the hatch door securely to the rest of the ship.

"Pull it tighter, doctor… that's good," he called, tying off a strap. Robbie was with them, one arm in a makeshift sling, but he used his good arm to check his work. "What do you think?" Jett asked. "If Duke jumps this through time, will it stay together?"

"The important bits, at least," Robbie shrugged, then winced at the movement. "Thanks, man. I'm not sure it's worth saving, but I'm definitely gonna try to fix it."

Dr. Emmett sloshed through the water to join them. "Valentine should be here soon, don't you think?"

Jett glanced at the sky, blinking the rain out of his eyes. "I would think so. I'm not sure how he's getting here, though. We're assuming he's a time-traveler, but we don't know how he does it."

"Let's wait for him inside," Robbie shivered. "No need to drown ourselves in all this rain."

Water splashed under their shoes and splattered over their clothes as they made their way to the *Starlight's* main door. Jett climbed up first before turning to give the other two men a hand. Since the ship was tilted, the door was high off the ground, and even if the boarding ramp would've helped Jett was pretty sure the mechanism behind it was smashed.

He checked on each of his friends, lit by the faint, gray light from outside. Duke had slept all night, and was still fast asleep in the corner, wrapped up in his damp suit coat. He looked dead and happy at the same time. Cariss was sitting by the control panel, quietly tinkering with it. Jett wasn't sure of what she was doing, but Robbie wasn't freaking out, so he guessed she wasn't harming the ship.

Anton sat on his own in the shadows, hypervigilant. It still felt surreal to have him on the ship. His curls were sticking to his brow with the inescapable wetness of Rendova. The gray light cast an icy, ethereal glow on him, and he looked young, yes, but there was something in his eyes that made Jett think of an older, tired man.

Parker was sitting with Tate, but she got up as they came in. "Dr. Emmett, I think he's waking up," she said. "He was mumbling something, but I can't understand him."

Jett followed the doctor to Tate's side. The makeshift bandage around the boy's head was caked to his scalp with dried blood. He looked up at them blearily, though one of his eyes was swollen shut. Jett was momentarily caught off guard by the diamond blue of his eye, and his mind told him in the same thought both that he was looking at Maddie and that he was looking at Anton.

"...Jett?" Tate said weakly, snapping him back to reality.

"He sounds worse than yesterday," Parker said worriedly. "Do you think he's concussed?"

"Almost definitely," Dr. Emmett said. "Thomas, who am I?"

"But... what?" Tate said. His hand traveled up to his head where the bandage was sticking to his wound. "What is this?"

"Your head is bleeding," the doctor said, slowly and clearly. "Do you remember why?"

"We were on Reka... right? Where are we?"

Jett knew next to nothing about injuries, but he guessed this regression in memory was a bad sign. "You'll remember," he said, hoping it was the truth. "Doctor, do you think he should try to sleep again?"

That seemed to awaken Tate, though his words were still jumbled. "Sleep! Do I have a concussion? What happened? Brain injury, you know, might be worse if I sleep, if I injured... you know. What happened?"

Dr. Emmett looked over the wound, his touch light and

experienced. "His head is still bleeding," he said, shaking his head. "I don't like this, not at all."

With great effort, Tate lifted his hand to his head. His words were slurred, but his brain seemed to be catching up to the situation. "Feels like a pretty bad scalp wound. The biggest concern is a skull fracture, of course. I don't think this was made by anything sharp, so I must've hit a dull surface hard enough that it broke the skin. There's possibly internal hemorrhage. Possibly concussed, but I'm speaking pretty well now. If I fall asleep, watch for changes in my breathing. In fact, don't let me sleep."

He talked about his wounds as if they were on a patient of his and not himself, and as if he expected everybody to understand what he was saying and what to do to help. Jett had never felt so ignorant. The swelling seemed to be spreading across the side of the boy's face.

"Tate, no need to self-diagnose," Dr. Emmett said, and Jett felt a surge of gratefulness for his presence. "I'm going to take care of you. Your face doesn't look good, but the swelling is on the outside, which is a good sign. But I don't ever like head swelling, not this far up. A skull won't stretch for swelling. If there's any inside, close to your brain, we're in for trouble. How's the pain?"

Tate winced. "Bad," he admitted. "But m'good."

He fell quiet, and then his face turned almost imperceptibly paler. Quick as a flash, Dr. Emmett shoved Jett aside and propped Tate up on his side. It was just in time, as the boy threw up instantly.

"I'll clean it up," Parker said, jumping up to do it.

"Are you okay, Tate?" Jett asked anxiously.

"I dunno," he said, eyeing his mess sheepishly. "I might be concussed. The bleeding in my head needs to stop, that'll make me feel better."

"Jett, keep him awake and take his bandage off. I'll find some cloth to redo it," Dr. Emmett said, scooting away to find something to work with. Jett knew it was selfish, but he hoped the doctor would find something other than his favorite jacket which he had carefully folded up and left in the only dry corner.

"Is there anything I can do?" he asked softly, carefully peeling the bandage off. Tate liked to keep his hair cropped short, but it was as brown and soft as Maddie's had been.

"My head... you know," Tate said vaguely, and he closed his eyes. "I'm a little dizzy. I need to elevate... you know... and how do my pupils look?"

"Like... pupils," Jett answered, just as vaguely. "I'm sorry, I'm a terrible doctor, I know."

"Yeah," Tate said, his eyes unfocused.

Jett began to panic. "Stay awake, son, come on!" he said, hovering over the boy. "Are you okay? Can you hear me?"

"What?" he slurred. His eyes closed.

Dr. Emmett hurried back, pressing his fingers to Tate's neck and lifting one of his eyelids with his thumb. "His pupils are enlarged," he murmured, pulling off his own coat. He rolled it up and pushed it under the boy's neck, elevating his head. He pressed his palms against his cheeks and then the back of his hand against his forehead. "He's cold, very cold. I need water, something he can eat, and something to staunch the bleeding."

"Use my coat," Parker offered, unzipping it. "It's a little wet, is that okay?"

"It's fine. I want you to cut the sleeves and the front off, and then I want you to take it outside and get it good and wet before bringing it to me. Jesse, is there a way you can get me drinking water?"

"Robbie has a water bottle somewhere," he answered, standing up.

Parker was butchering her coat with her pocket knife like a pro. Jett dashed across the room and came back with the water. Dr. Emmett took it, poured some of it into the boy's mouth and then pushed his finger down his throat, forcing him to swallow. Tate spluttered and blinked, but then his eyes rolled back and he fainted again.

Parker hurried outside, and came back a moment later with her hair dripping and her coat soaking wet in her hand. "There's some kind of light outside," she said, handing it to the doctor. She looked at Jett, and he could see the concern in her lopsided frown. "It almost looks like somebody has a fire going."

Cariss looked up with stony eyes, and she got up and walked to the door with eerie calmness. She gazed out for several moments before speaking. "Duke," she said, "we have a problem."

Duke woke up at the sound of his name. "Huh?"

"I see fire," she said.

Jett glanced from one to the other. "That's not a big deal, is it? Do you think there's people out there?"

"No people. Just fire," Cariss said.

Duke scrambled to his feet, looking around wildly like a caged animal.

Parker shook her head. "Why are you worried about fire? We're literally sitting in a soaked ship on the wettest island there ever was."

"...And that's why we're worried, thanks for summing that up," Cariss said. The door was propped up in the doorway, and she shoved it as shut as it would go; then jerked off her coat, dropped it and kicked it into a puddle that had formed in the doorway.

Duke dug through the storage compartments. "Come on, Robbie, don't you have anything useful in here? Blankets, towels, emergency ponchos?"

"I took most of my stuff out before I went to Reka," the pilot answered, eyeing him. "But whaddya want an emergency poncho for? There's no way you're gonna dry off anytime soon."

"I estimate we have sixty seconds before it gets here," Cariss said. "The door doesn't close, and we're standing in rainwater. Doctor, you need to move Thomas away from the door."

"Guys, what are you talking about? There's no way we should be freaking out about fire," Parker said. She marched over to the door and peered out. Jett heard her gasp. "Oh my goodness."

He joined her at the door. Across the grove was a burst of color: orange and yellow against the blue and gray of the island. It was fire, jumping and skipping across the sand, riding the flood and wrapping around the trees. It latched onto leaves, and they shriveled into nothing as it sucked out all of the moisture. Even trees crumbled at its touch.

"Duke," Jett said slowly, "What is that?"

"It's my mother's invention," he said, sounding defeated. "It's not real fire, of course, I think it's actually some kind of chemical compound that feeds on water."

"Is it harmful?" Dr. Emmett asked. "Is it capable of burning things?"

Duke swallowed. "It's meant to melt oceans. If you're wet, it'll burn you."

"Aren't humans, like, sixty percent water or something?" Robbie asked.

"Thanks, Robbie, that's exactly what we wanted to hear," Parker said, grabbing the door and trying to pull it into place.

"I need your coat," Duke said, and Jett glanced over, almost expecting him to be holding the North Face jacket. Instead, he was looking at Robbie. "It's damp, but I can still use it to mop up the floor."

"We've got rain coming in through at least seven different places," Parker pointed out. "I don't think drying the floor is gonna do any good!"

Jett turned in a circle, eyeing the layout of the ship. "The floor is tilted. Is it any drier on the higher end?"

"Water is coming in from that way, too," Cariss said. "It would be like sitting under a waterfall."

"Bad idea, then," he muttered.

"And… sixty seconds is up," Cariss said.

A wave of heat slapped against the ship. Flames licked the doorway. Dr. Emmett jumped in front of Tate, shielding him from the fire. Jett hurried toward them, sliding across the tilted floor. He grabbed the unconscious boy by the shoulders and with the doctor's help he dragged him back. The fire danced away and the heat receded.

"That really stings," Dr. Emmett gasped, supporting himself against the wall. The back of his arm and neck were an angry red.

"It's coming back!" Parker yelled.

"The control panels feel dry," Cariss said.

"Get up there, then!" Duke shouted, grabbing her and half pushing, half lifting her up.

Robbie climbed up behind her, using his good arm to keep from sliding off. Jett tried to lift Tate, but he could tell right away that it wasn't going to work. Thankfully, Duke and Parker gave him a hand, and together they hefted the boy onto the panels. "It's really slanted up here," Parker noted, climbing up. "I'll keep Tate from sliding off, don't worry."

"We're not all going to fit up here," Cariss noted. "I estimate that six of us can. If there's a dry jacket or surface two of us can hide behind, I recommend we find it quickly."

"I can find something," Dr. Emmett began, but Jett shook his head.

"Get up there, uncle! I've got my jacket, let me find it."

Duke helped the doctor up and Jett turned to find his jacket, but to his horror he saw Anton on the far side of the ship. He stood, rain falling onto his face and water rushing between his feet, gazing at the door with morbid fascination. The fire poked around the entrance. Its light reflected off of every shiny surface in the *Starlight*, making Anton the center of a bubble of light.

As the fire leapt in, Jett threw himself against Anton, sending both of them crashing against the wall. He fumbled with his jacket and covered them both. Internally, his thoughts were screaming *save her save her don't let Maddie die*, and though he knew it was his son and not his wife he clung to him tightly, reassured by the warmth of his skin and the rise and fall of his breathing.

He felt a wave of smothering, wet heat, and he almost laughed. *I survived the Red Planet to die like this,* he thought. *And I was so sure I could actually go home.* The heat intensified, and Anton shuddered against him and he thought he heard Parker screaming. His mind wandered to Logan, who was probably drawing more pictures of him in space with construction paper and crayons. He thought of Janet the babysitter, who was undoubtedly going to quit her job with all of the extra hours he made her work.

He thought of his coworkers, and he wondered how he was supposed to explain Teddy's disappearance. He imagined his friends and family watching his sudden friendship with Tate Emmett, and wondering what had caused it. He pictured his house in his mind, but instead of how small and sad it usually looked, the spare room had been cleaned up and he was offering Anton a place to stay.

His shoes weren't under the protection of his jacket, and the fire was latching onto his socks, searching for the skin beneath them to turn into ash. Somehow it got hotter, and though he could barely breathe he pulled the jacket even tighter and pulled Anton even closer. In his make-believe world, he spent more time with Logan, and Parker offered to watch him sometimes. He was helping with Tate's college payments, and he listened to him explain complicated procedures and surgeries as if he actually understood.

At this point he was pretty sure the air he was breathing was fire. His skin was dry and clammy and feverish, and his throat and lungs felt like sandpaper. It continued for one more agonizing moment, and then the fire fell back, chasing the rain. The heat eased up a little and he hacked out a cough, clinging to his jacket and his son with no intention of moving.

15

A Little Curiosity

A hand shook his shoulder, and he winced at the sting. "Jett, are you okay?" Parker demanded. She pulled the jacket away and gray light hit his eyes. He sat up, blinking, and started coughing.

"The fire could be back any moment," she said, looking at him worriedly. "Was the jacket enough to keep you safe?"

"I think it shielded us from the worst of it," he croaked, glancing at Anton. The jacket was partly obscuring his face still, but as far as he could see the boy looked fine. They both had red and inflamed patches wherever their skin had been exposed, but the sting was dying away quickly.

"Anything dry repels it," Duke explained. "The panels are dry enough that it didn't get close to us, but it got fairly close to you. Parker, you're sitting in water. Get back up here before it comes back."

"I don't see it anymore," she said, looking at the door. "Maybe it moved on?"

She walked toward the doorway and Duke looked to be on the verge of passing out with anxiety. Jett wrapped the jacket around Anton, pushing the boy's arms through the sleeves. "Keep this on," he ordered, "and stay back here." He sloshed through the water to join Parker at the door.

"There's nothing out there," she said. "I think it's on the other side of the ship."

"Let me check," Jett said, pushing past her. "We need to know if it's still close enough to be a concern. Stay here."

He stepped out and his shoes sank several inches in water. Stubbornly, Parker followed him. They crept around the *Starlight*, waiting for the hot flash of the flames. Jett peered around the corner, and then jumped, startled.

"Valentine," he gasped. "You scared me."

The man was on the other side of the ship, eyeing the wreckage. He was wearing a suit and his usual obnoxious tie, and his hands were pushed deep into his pockets. "Did you get here a day early?" he asked, grinning.

Jett sighed. "Duke's calculations were off. He said the portal leads to today, but we got here yesterday. If that makes any sense. Time-travel, you know."

"That's a shame. You didn't catch Rendova at its best," he said, "unless you're a fan of tropical cyclones."

"Did you do something with the fire?" Parker asked, looking around warily.

Valentine gave a dramatic sweep of his hand. "That, my observant lady, is an excellent question. I made a portal and sent it right back to where it came from."

"So it's gone?" Jett asked.

"Yes. Duke's mother is probably chasing it again in the Nova Atlantis bay."

Jett realized he was shaking. His heart was thudding like a drum and he was *shaking*, hard and uncontrollably. He clung to the side of the ship and took a deep breath, trying to let the adrenaline run its course. He heard water splashing behind him and he saw Duke, his hand on the gun in his suit jacket. He relaxed slightly when he saw Valentine, but he kept his hand where it was.

"Are you a time-traveler? Is it a machine or your own ability?" he demanded. His eyes were kindling.

Valentine laughed, and there was a strange and frightening power in it. "Me, a time-traveler! Imagine the fun I'd have with that. I'd travel through history, I would, and lay out a picnic blanket and watch the fun. I'd watch the dawn of time and the last sunset of sunsets. I'd let ancient civilizations soar in rockets, and I'd take the children of the future to unravel the secrets of the past." He dropped his volume and bared his teeth. "If I could time-travel, the fun would never end."

"I can feel it," Duke breathed. He sounded like he'd had the wind knocked out of him. "I can *feel* your power. Why did I never feel it before?"

"I never let you," Valentine shrugged. "There's so much more you could learn about your abilities if you weren't so busy catering to Channyng."

"But how long have you known that I could time-travel?"

"Since the explosion. I sensed it right away," Valentine said. "You hid it pretty well, though. I was under the impression you didn't actually *do* anything with it. Mr. Duke, you've only scraped the surface of what you're capable of. The portal I made in the bay? That's real power."

"That was a hole through time and space, an invitation for accidents and paradoxes," Duke argued. "For goodness' sake, why'd you put one there anyway?"

The man shrugged. "I wanted to bring one of my boats here, and that called for a portal in the ocean. I didn't realize anybody would be on that beach anytime soon. Don't worry, I closed it. But Duke, have you ever heard of Angel's Crypt? It has connections to time-travel, I just know it."

"I don't know anything about it."

"Have you ever looked into the future, to see what you become?" Valentine asked. "It's an incredible gift you've been given, and you do next to nothing with it. I looked. Someday, you're going to be known as the Man who froze time."

"I'm afraid I don't know what that means."

"You never will unless you embrace what you are. Stop hiding in Channyng's shadow. You're a better, more powerful man than he is."

Duke shook his head, still gripping his gun. "I've seen a piece of my future, and I don't like it. I don't want to be another Johnson."

"Can we discuss this later?" Parker interrupted. "Tate's badly injured, and we need a plan. Are we going back to Nova Atlantis?"

Jett rubbed his hands together. "Has anyone considered taking us straight back to Nebraska?"

"No, let me take you to my house," Valentine pleaded. "I won't keep you for long, and I know a doctor who has everything you could possibly need to patch up your friend, and he's an expert at keeping his mouth shut."

"I'll talk to Dr. Emmett about it. What would we do with the *Starlight*?" Duke asked, clearly not pleased with the idea.

"You could take it back to the docking bay in Nova Atlantis, and I'll take everyone else," offered Valentine. "Channyng's expecting you."

"I'm going to talk with Emmett. I'll be back," Duke said, heading towards the ship.

"Send Anton out, will you?" the man called after him.

Duke shot back a mutinous glare before disappearing inside. Chuckling under his breath, Valentine swaggered through the small clearing, looking at the tropical foliage with interest. The rain clouds were slowly letting up, giving way to a gray, watery sky and a splash of sunlight.

Jett eyed him warily, thinking of past conversations. "You know a lot more about us than you're letting on, don't you?" he asked.

Valentine shot him one of his famous publicity smiles. "Perhaps," he said.

Duke came back. By now, his dress shoes that had undoubtedly cost a fortune were a wet, lost cause. "Emmett wants to speak with you," he said, his eyes flickering moodily. "Come inside, but don't touch anything."

"I wouldn't dream of it," the man said dramatically, following him inside.

The moment they were gone, Parker shook her head. "Nova Atlantis is run by a pack of selfish children," she ranted.

"Couldn't agree more," Jett answered. He took in the brightening sky, the black sand and the extensive puddles. "I guess we'll have to take his word for it that the fire's gone. I wonder if this island is ever dry."

Parker gazed at the trees, and Jett could hear the underlying excitement in her voice. "I think I can hear the ocean. Can you hear it?"

"I'm not sure," he said. "I'm guessing it's close, though. I'm also guessing you want to look for it?"

"Yes!" she said eagerly. "I love the ocean."

"If we get lost, I'm blaming you," he said warningly, and she laughed. Together they navigated around trees and thick bushes, following the growing sound of the ocean. Jett knew very little about the sea, so when they came across a steep incline he wondered if they were going in the wrong direction. However, Parker pushed forward confidently, so he let her take the lead and they climbed up the hill.

As they climbed, he couldn't help but think of what Dr. Emmett had said on Reka. *'A brave, pretty girl... I bet she'd love to meet Logan.'* Trying to look past his uncle's blatant matchmaking, he wondered if there was an actual reason for his saying it. Yes, she was brave and pretty and yes, she'd probably like Logan, but then again she liked everyone except for adults who behaved like selfish children, apparently.

If there was something bigger that had prompted Dr. Emmett to say it, Jett wanted to know. He knew that the doctor was usually right in his judgments of character. If he thought that Jett and Parker would be good together, well, he was probably right. But personally, Jett was struggling to see it. Parker could probably make anybody happy. He, on the other hand, was a stick in the mud who missed his dead wife and he knew it.

"It's beautiful," Parker said, interrupting his train of thought. They had reached the top of the hill, and were now standing on a sort of cliff overlooking the sea. It was very unlike the stormy beach of Nova Atlantis. While that beach had felt like a used sock, worn through and uncared for, Rendova shone with a wild, untamed brilliance. The ocean was a vivid blue, the sand was a solid black, and the green and brown of the trees contributed to the sharp color contrasts. It was still raining, just barely, which made the place smell strongly of sand and freshness.

"I wish I could draw it. I had a little sketchpad in my coat pocket, but it's definitely soaked by now," Parker said mournfully. "I'm terrible at remembering things to paint later. The moment I walk away from something I forget what it looks like."

Jett shrugged. "I could probably remember. I can sketch it out for you."

Her eyes lit up. "You like sketching?"

He shook his hand in the so-so motion. "Teddy and Maddie used to make me draw out their inventions for them since I was the only one who was any good at it. Don't ask me to do anything with paint or color, though, or you'll be disappointed."

"I love painting," she said enthusiastically. "I'm not very good at sketching, though I'm trying to get better at it. Tate's good at it, so I'm guessing he gets it from you. Can you draw people? You should see the mess I make of hands and fingers, it's embarrassing."

Jett laughed. "I used to draw Logan a lot. Just sketches."

"You'll have to show me sometime," she said.

He gave a noncommittal shrug. They stood side by side, letting the moments pass by, quiet beside the murmur of the ocean.

Parker rubbed her arms, trying to warm herself up, though with the awkwardness of her movements it looked more like she was fidgeting. The slight frown on her face added to her nervous look. "I'm sorry," she blurted suddenly.

He raised an eyebrow, waiting for her to explain.

"About Duke," she clarified, hugging herself. "He's not who I thought he was. When he came to Nebraska, he was so set on finding you and setting the paradox right. I know I shouldn't have, but I believed everything he said."

Jett tilted his head. "So did I. What's the issue?"

"He lies, he loses his temper, and he throws fits like a child," she said vehemently. "I haven't known him for much longer than I've known you, but I was perfectly willing to follow him anywhere he asked. I thought he was some kind of hero, and I wanted to be a part of that."

"He's certainly a little different than what my first impression led me to believe," Jett said. "But not necessarily in a bad way. If anything, now that we've seen his home, he seems a little more... human."

She blinked. "Maybe," she relented, "but I shouldn't have agreed to join his team until I knew who he really was."

"I'd agree with that," Jett said. "But you played a big role in convincing me to find Tate and Anton, so I'd say something good came out of it."

"Really?" she said, looking hopeful.

"Sure," he answered.

She gave a lopsided smile, but it quickly melted away. "What's that?" she asked, pointing.

He faced the ocean. On the beach, large, sprawling letters were drawn in the sand, taking up several square feet. Jett squinted, trying to make sense of the words. It was difficult to see from their distance.

Curious, Parker scrambled down the cliff, and Jett followed close behind her. She jumped over the last few feet of the climb, landing with a soft *thud* in the sand. "I didn't see anybody over here," she said, approaching the patch of sand. "Who wrote this?"

"I don't know," Jett said, walking around it, being careful to not step on any of the letters. He stepped back and tilted his head. It was large, sprawling handwriting, making him think somehow of fire and ash. It was a strange poem that he might have laughed at back in Nebraska, but on the enigma that was Rendova Island there seemed to be something sinister about it.

The dead will whisper what will be:
The past, the present, perishing.
The Friend, the Foe, has caused a rift,
The Rift, the Secret - Angel's Crypt.

"It's just a silly poem," Parker said.

"It's about Angel's Crypt," Jett said. His heart sank. "Parker, we can't tell anyone about this. You have no idea what people would do to find this."

"But it's just a poem!"

"King!" they heard Valentine yell. His voice was close, too close. "You're going to be sorry if I ruin my suit looking for you. Designer brands aren't cheap!"

"Cover it up!" Jett whispered, kicking at the poem. His shoes left gashes across the damp sand. "We can't let Valentine know we saw this. He's gonna assume I wrote it and buried treasure here."

"Stop!" Parker exclaimed, grabbing his arm. He ignored her, stretching out his foot to get the rest of the words. "Stop, what are you doing?"

"I'll explain later," he said, smoothing out the last letters. "We're right here!" he called, loud enough for Valentine to hear. "We're coming!"

"I've already forgotten what it said," Parker said, angry. "What is wrong with you? You destroyed something that is probably super important!"

"It's not worth the trouble, believe me. You don't want to get mixed up in all of that."

"I think you're mistaking me for you," she shot back. "Some people aren't actually scared of having a little curiosity."

"Curiosity rarely ends well!"

"Of course *you'd* say that!"

Jett blinked. "What's that supposed to mean?"

"I have literally never met a man with as little curiosity or motivation to experience new things as you."

He shrugged. "I see no problem with that. My life in Nebraska has always been more than enough for me."

"We're hundreds of years in the future, experiencing

things that no one else ever will, and you're still pretending you can go home like none of this ever happened!"

"That's the whole point of me wanting to go home, Parker! I don't want to put time-travel into my daily routine!"

She marched towards the cliff and Valentine's voice, turning her back on him. "Don't bother talking to *me*, then. I don't think I'd fit very well in your schedule!"

"Parker!" he said, sprinting to catch up with her. "Look, there's no reason for us to be mad at each other."

"You shouldn't have erased the poem," she said. She walked briskly, keeping her eyes on the treeline.

"It was for your own good. Look, if you knew that poem, you'd be sucked into a whole plot to solve riddles and find some legendary crypt with some kind of treasure in it that is very possibly time-travel."

"And what if that's what I wanted?"

He jogged to keep up with her, though he had the distinct impression that Parker wouldn't let him catch up in her present mood. "I'm sorry. I wanted to make sure you knew what you were getting into first."

"I get it, King. I'm not allowed to want adventure."

Valentine was waiting for them at the top of the hill, and he looked amused when he saw their expressions. "Something wrong?" he asked, glancing from one to the other.

"No," they answered simultaneously.

Valentine looked like he very much doubted their answer, but wisely he dropped it. "We're ready to go back to Nova Atlantis. Duke is taking the *Starlight* to the dock, and I'm taking the rest of you straight to my house. Follow me."

The three of them made their way back to the ship. Jett reviewed the scene at the beach in his mind, trying to find where he had gone wrong. Parker was making it a point not to look at him. The silence was strained, and for the first time Jett wished Valentine would say something, just to cover it up.

16

Second Most Powerful

Duke leaned against the *Starlight's* doorway. He watched the doctor get Tate ready to move. "I hope we're making the right decision," Emmett said, carefully adjusting the bandage. "If we don't get the medical treatment Valentine promised us, we need to go back to Nebraska, or I don't know that he'll make it."

"Understood," he promised. "If you grab his legs, I'll help you carry him out."

The doctor nodded and helped him pick up Tate, staunchly bearing half the weight. It was a bit of a struggle to get over the tilted floor and through the door, but fortunately the boy wasn't heavy. As they stepped outside, they saw Valentine returning with Jett and Parker in tow.

"You're gonna want to see this, Mr. Duke," Valentine said, rolling up his sleeves. "Before I take them back, I'm going to give you a show of what real power is."

Duke sighed, laying Tate down in the sand. "I'm afraid I'll have to pass on your offer. I need to get the *Starlight* back."

Cariss was going with him, and she was already waiting

in the ship. Robbie was leaning against a tree, cradling his arm. Dr. Emmett was fussing over Tate like he'd been doing for most of the time they'd spent on Rendova, too absorbed in the boy's safety to spare much of his time for the others. Anton was off to the side, wrapped up in Jett's jacket, eyeing everyone with a heavy glare of distrust.

Valentine swaggered up to Duke, holding out his hand. "Then I guess this is goodbye for now," he said. "We'll have to catch up later, though. I know you hate me but that doesn't mean we can't be friends."

As much as he didn't want to, Duke reached out to return the shake. The moment they grasped hands, his eyes blazed and his senses burned. The familiar, golden glow emanated from his hands.

"Stop!" he said, trying to pull his hand away. "You're going to make me shift to another point in time!"

"I'm helping you feel your power," Valentine said, keeping him in a tight grip. "Look, Mr. Duke. Can't you see it? Time is like a river, but instead of being swept along with the current, we're the water. We can go anywhere, see anywhere, be anywhere. Look carefully. What do you see?"

Duke blinked. The landscape around him changed. His friends faded away, replaced by howling winds and trees bending with the power of the storm. Rain was falling in thick sheets, but though he could see it he couldn't feel it at all. "This is yesterday," he gasped. "But I'm not really here, am I? I'm just looking at it."

"Have you ever done this before?" Valentine asked. "Stood in one moment and looked at another?"

"No. Not like this," he admitted. "Am I actually seeing this myself, or are you making me see it?"

The man grinned. "A bit of both. Look further. What do you see?"

Duke frowned. The landscape changed around him constantly, giving him a headache; all at once he was watching the sun rise and set a thousand times, the rain start and stop, the trees growing and dying. His eyes widened when he saw men dressed as soldiers darting across the sand, oblivious to his presence.

"Where are we now, World War 2?" he guessed.

"You can see Kennedy if you try, if you remember him from the history books. He stood here once," Valentine said, watching the scene play out with interest. "He was stationed on this island, stopping Japanese supply ships I believe, and his boat, the 109, was torn in two by a destroyer. It's a fairly riveting story."

The soldiers were gone just as quickly as they had appeared. Nausea rose in Duke's stomach, and he felt like his brain was being run through a wringer. His eyes watered, and though he fought to keep them open, he found that there was a measure of relief to be found in closing them. "Help me stop this," he said through gritted teeth. "We're making a rift in time."

"You're just looking, Mr. Duke. You're not actually time-traveling."

"We're still causing time disturbance!" Duke snapped, squeezing his eyes closed. "I'm really sensitive to time disturbance. I need you to stop!"

"It hurts at first, but I think you can do it with practice," Valentine encouraged.

The pain intensified. His stomach curdled, and there was a dull ache in his skull that was growing with every second. "Stop," he pleaded, his voice cracking. Though his eyes were shut, he could sense the island changing and fluctuating as time swept by. The torture grew, and he fell to his knees, pressing his free hand against his face. "You're going to kill me. I can't do this! Stop, please stop!"

Valentine released his hand. Instantly the pain receded, leaving him a shaking mess. He was on his knees in the sand, and as he opened his eyes he was relieved to see that the painful images were gone, replaced by the *Starlight* and his friends. Parker looked concerned, and Robbie hovered behind him.

"I'm okay, Robbie," he rasped. His throat was strangely sore. "I just shifted out of time. Nothing new."

"You were glowing, yeah, but you never actually disappeared," Robbie said, offering his good arm.

Duke accepted it and hefted himself to his feet. He looked at Valentine distrustfully. "So that was all in my head."

"There's a lot in your head, if you'd only look at it," the man said.

Duke shook himself, watching the last bit of golden light fade away. "I'll ask Channyng about it," he said stiffly. "But personally, I think this kind of power is too much for me or for you. I wish the world could be rid of it."

"Are you wishing me dead, Mr. Duke?" Valentine asked with a wry smile.

"I'll see you in Nova Atlantis, sir," Duke said. He turned away.

"Not the answer I was hoping for," Valentine chuckled. "You do work for Channyng, so I'll watch my back from now on. The man's a killer, so it would make sense that you're like him."

Duke ignored him and climbed into the *Starlight*.

He sank against the wall. Cariss poked and prodded at the panels, doing a final check on the field displacer. She had glanced up as he came in, but had gone back to her work without a word. The two of them were alone.

Sharp pain jolted through Duke's head. "Valentine must have made his portal," he winced. "I don't know how he manages the things he does. It hurts too much for me to even get close."

Cariss remained silent. She had his watch and she used it to check the key, making sure it was unharmed and ready for the time jump.

The pain faded, and he knew that Valentine and the others were gone. The man's parting words, however, lurked in the empty ship, taunting him. *Are you wishing me dead, Mr. Duke? Channyng's a killer, it would make sense you're like him. Channyng's a killer. You're like him.*

Duke saw Dr. Simons, babbling about his radios. He saw him questioning how Duke got around, and then he saw him on a police report with vacant eyes. *Channyng's a killer.*

Duke saw Valentine, pressing numbers into a keypad. He saw him dragging Anton away from bullets, begging Jett to save him, serious for once. *Are you wishing me dead, Mr. Duke?*

Duke saw Parker, wearing a white dress, and Robbie in a suit and tie. He saw Jett on the floor, dead. Murdered. *It would make sense you're like him.*

His gag reflex kicked in, and he dry heaved, clutching his stomach. He knelt over the floor and he saw a puddle with his reflection.

There was the shaky outline of his jaw, cheekbones, and his headful of chestnut hair. He was a normal person until he looked into his eyes. He knew what he'd see, but it hurt just as much to see it as it had ten years before. His iris was a fiery orange band that flickered and burned across the surface of the water. These days, he barely remembered what he was supposed to look like.

He didn't know why or how the next words tumbled out of his mouth, but he was powerless to stop them. "I'm going to kill somebody."

Cariss didn't seem perturbed. "Extra points if it's Channyng."

"It's going to be a good man," Duke said. "I'm going to snap and take an innocent man's life."

She shrugged, continuing her work. "I know you think your anger is uncontrollable, but I don't believe you'll ever go that far. I have faith that you're a better man than that."

"If I ever did snap," Duke said, "Would you forgive me?"

She shook her head. "No," she said. "I don't generally trust people. But I made the choice to trust you. If you betray that trust, you'll lose me."

"And then what would I do?" he asked. His voice was hollow.

"Then you might as well give up Parker, Robbie, and all the rest of them. If you drop to the level of a murderer, you're no better than Johnson or any of the scum that makes up Nova Atlantis. But I know you're better."

He gazed at the back of Cariss' long, graying hair, and grinned. Looking down he saw his eyes reflected in the puddle, burning with ill-concealed despair. "Thanks," he said. "I'm glad to know where I stand."

She turned, tilting her head as she took him in. "Are you well?"

He laughed and pushed himself to his feet. "Never been better," he said. "Let's get out of here. I've got work to do."

She eyed him, but then she double checked her calculations and pulled a lever. The ship jolted and the next moment they were scraping into their former spot in the docking bay.

The door was still clinging to the rest of the ship. Duke kicked it and it fell off its hinges, clattering onto the metal walkway like a gangplank. He strode out, leaving Cariss behind to shut things down and close things up.

Security officers were strolling around the dock, talking on their radios and checking behind gates. As the *Starlight's* gate swung open, several of them came running, their guns at the ready.

"Hands behind your head!" one of them shouted.

Duke stopped. "Please, put down your weapons and get out of my way," he said. The fire in his eyes flickered dangerously.

"Uh, no way," the officer answered. "You were the last

person seen with Anton Venedict, and we're under orders to bring him in by whatever means necessary."

"You won't find Anton. I know exactly where he is, yes, but I'm not going to tell you," he said calmly, "because I have every intention of bringing him in myself. So lower your guns and get lost."

The officer hesitated. "I'm not sure you have the proper authority for that order."

Duke shook his head. "Then you don't know who you're talking to," he said. "I'm Channyng's PA, which in most people's opinion would make me the second most powerful person in this city."

Cariss hurried out of the *Starlight's* gate, holding out his watch. He took it from her and slapped it onto his wrist while she eyed the officers, taking in their situation. "Are we under arrest?" she asked.

"No," he said calmly. "If you're with me, you're on the right side."

A trace of concern peeked out the cracks of her stony expression. "Duke, what are you doing?"

"We can't permit you to leave," one of the officers interrupted. "If you refuse to obey our orders, we'll have to resort to force."

Duke pressed a few buttons on his watch and lifted his wrist. Everyone frowned, including Cariss, and they watched him warily. The watch beeped once, and then started a voice call. Channyng answered immediately. "Hello?"

"Channyng," Duke said, "I know where Anton is, but

Security won't let me out of the dock. Could you give them a message?"

Channyng's smile could be heard clearly in his voice. "It would be my pleasure," he said, his voice sickly sweet. "Tell them that whoever is in charge is fired. I don't care who it is."

The officers gasped, lowering their weapons. A murmur of protest began, but Duke lifted his hand for silence and Channyng raised his voice. "You're getting off easy. I've done a lot to make your jobs as comfortable as they can be, and how do you repay me? You lose Anton and you heckle my favorite gardener. I could have every one of your badges, I could have your families deported, and I could take away your citizenship in this city. But am I doing any of that? No. So go home with grateful hearts and good jobs. Nobody is ever allowed to stand in Mr. Duke's way, you know that."

The officers didn't need a second warning. There was an unorganized scramble for their vans as they beat a hasty retreat.

"Thank you," Duke said quietly.

"No problem," Channyng said. "You don't generally let me do that sort of thing for you; it was fun. But do you really know where Anton is?"

"I can do you even better. Do you still want to see Jett King and his friends?"

"You've got my full attention."

"Does tomorrow work?"

Channyng hummed. "No. That's the presentation, remember? It'll be a late night. I'd love to see them first thing the day after, though. You know where I live."

"What are you talking about?" Cariss hissed.

Duke ignored her. "I'll bring them," he promised. "Good-bye, sir."

"See ya."

Duke ended the call. Briskly he walked down the walkway, the metal beneath him *clanking* with each step. He was fully aware of how wet and bedraggled he looked, but the rage that was building inside of him made him walk with bitter confidence, ignoring the never-ending looks thrown his way. Cariss trailed behind him, but he tried to push her out of his mind. *If I'm going to lose her*, he thought to himself, half-hysterical, *it might as well be on my own terms.*

17

Honesty

Jett never wanted to go through a portal again.

Firstly because it was invisible. Valentine said "follow me," and he did, but when he took a step the sand gave way beneath his feet and he was falling through nothing, and he landed on a hardwood floor on his face. To make it worse, he'd been fighting off a terrible headache since then as well as occasional bouts of dizziness. His friends were mostly fine, except for Robbie, who threw up and said he'd rather have fallen through a cheese grater.

Jett, Dr. Emmett, Tate, Anton, Robbie and Parker were led through Valentine's house. It was spacious and well laid out, but the defining feature was the abundance of books. Being the 23rd century, where digital copies were the handiest, the man was obviously quite the collector. Bookshelves lined the walls and stood in random corners, and in some places the books were piled on the floor.

Besides that, there were awards, plaques, and medals on display, all bearing the name *Ernest R. Valentine III, Esquire*. A screen was built into the wall, playing a televised debate on the role of ethics in science.

"Julia!" Valentine called in a sing-song voice. Immediately, she poked her head out of a doorway. Her curly brown hair was smothered by the headset she wore, which had a large speaking device covering her face.

"Jett! Good to see you again," she said warmly. "Oh my, what happened to Tate? Ernest, do you need me to...?"

"Yes," he said in answer to her unspoken question. "Call Moon. That man's a miracle worker."

"I'll introduce myself to all of you later!" she said. She shot them a smile that was all pearly teeth before disappearing.

Valentine smiled fondly. "As you know, Jett, she works for Security."

"Yes, I distinctly remember getting arrested by her," he said dryly.

Valentine laughed and pushed open another door. "Put the injured kid in here," he instructed. "Emmett, once my friend gets here you've got nothing to worry about. He's the Head of Health and Safety at the Space Agency, and nobody's better at their job."

They carried Tate into the room, laying him out on the bed. "Everybody seems to work for the Space Agency," Robbie commented. "Are there even any other ones?"

"The Space Agency is by far the biggest and most influential," Valentine said. "If you're one of the Heads there, you're practically royalty in this city. There's no money or notoriety in the other agencies. Channyng, Dr. Tyler-Duke, me and all the other Heads... everybody wants to either be us or kill us."

"This sounds like a downright lovely place to live," Robbie said.

Valentine merely winked. "Dr. Emmett, once my friend gets here he'll probably want to move Tate to his place, and I'm guessing you'll want to go with him. As for the rest of you, you can come with me."

"Wait a moment," Dr. Emmett said. "Who is your doctor friend? He can't really be the Head of Health and Safety, because that would mean he's Dr. Moon."

"So you've heard a little bit about... our disagreements," Valentine surmised.

"Disagreements is too weak a word," Dr. Emmett said. "When I was at Duke's house I looked over a few headlines, and the most numerous were about you and Dr. Moon. According to reporters, you've tried to have each other assassinated several times. You argue with everything the other says, and you make it very clear that you despise each other."

"I saw a great headline about us the other day: *The Best Entertainment We've Had Since the Tyler-Dukes*," Valentine said proudly.

"So it can't be him," Dr. Emmett reasoned.

"It seems our reputation precedes us," Valentine said. "But you're wrong. It is certainly Dr. Moon from the SA that I'm talking about."

Emmett frowned. "I don't think I understand."

"There are many things about this city that you don't understand," Valentine said, and his smile felt oddly warm. "You looked at the headlines and all you saw was hate, treachery, greed, and hunger. But the headlines won't tell you the truth.

And, yes, I believe there still is some truth in this city, along with love and friendship and courage. We just don't make the news."

Dr. Emmett didn't look too sure, but Valentine didn't give him a chance to say anything else. He walked out of the room. Jett exchanged a look with his uncle before following, along with Parker, Robbie and Anton.

As Valentine showed them around, Jett began to realize how big the house really was. Each room was full of everything from beds to antiques to books to an indoor pool and garden to ridiculous amounts of clothes, but hardly any of it felt used or lived in. It made him think of rich people who simply didn't know what to do with all of their wealth.

It did feel nice, if slightly overwhelming, to be given his own room with a private bathroom and shower. He even found an entire pack of unused toothbrushes. He took his time, washing away the smell of smoke and seawater and the filth of sand and mud. Thankfully there were clothes small enough to fit him, though he felt strangely cold without his jacket. He knew Anton was in the room beside his, and he considered going over and asking if he could have it back before thinking better of it.

He combed his hair and mourned the fact that since he was in the 23rd century, his favorite barber was dead and buried somewhere. It felt odd to think that *he* was dead and buried somewhere, his life over long ago. He pushed the morbid thought from his head, finished his hair and found a pair of shoes to put on.

There was a knock on his door, and he hurried to answer

it. It was Valentine. "Moon is here," he said, "and he's about to move Tate. He woke up, so I thought maybe you'd like to see him before he goes."

"Yes, of course," Jett said. He glanced at Anton's door, making a mental note to check on him as soon as possible, and then followed Valentine down the hall. When they got to Tate's room, the man hung back, but Jett slipped through the partially open door.

Tate was still on the bed, wearing damp, muddy clothes and covered in bloody bandages. A pale man with glasses and dark hair was digging through what looked like a medical bag, and Dr. Emmett was watching him like a hawk.

The pale man looked up as he came in. "I assume you're Jesse King," he said. "I'm pleased to make your acquaintance at last. You may call me Moon."

"Do you think you can help Tate?" Jett asked.

The doctor gave a nod. "I'm certain of it. Medicine is far more advanced in this century than it was in yours; this is nothing."

Jett frowned. "So you know we got here by time-travel."

"I know everything that Valentine knows. Including your possible connection to Angel's Crypt. If you know anything that you'd like to share..."

"I get it, I get it, I'll pass it along," Jett said, waving him off. He sat down in a chair next to the bed. "How are you doing, Tate?"

The boy looked at him blearily. His eye was still swollen shut. "I'm okay," he said. "This has not been fun, but I'm okay."

He was definitely putting on a brave front. "I'm so sorry you got hurt," Jett said. "I'll do my best to get you home safely."

"I know," Tate said drowsily. "Where's Anton? He's lying, you know."

Jett frowned, raising a brow. "Valentine gave him a room. What do you mean, he's lying?"

"I dunno," Tate said. "Remember how I can kind of hear him in my head? Well, ever since we actually met each other it's been so much louder. I think I could talk to him through my head if I really tried. Right now I can hear his thoughts, and I'm pretty sure he's coming up with a good lie."

"Why would Anton need to lie?"

Tate shrugged. "Beats me. But he doesn't like you. He hates that he makes you think of a mother he doesn't know anything about and that you took him away from Johnson." He winced, rubbing his head. "I didn't mean to say that. I think he thought that just now."

Jett gaped, momentarily speechless. He remembered saying that Anton looked like his mother, but he hadn't considered that Anton had no idea of who his mother was and what she had looked like. For the first time he wondered how Anton had known that he was his father, and realized that he must have learned during his time on the *Kenswick*. He was reminded of the absurdity of the situation; he had two almost grown sons, not much younger than he was, who had both grown up entirely without him.

"Do you... do you know anything about your mother?" he said hesitantly. "You grew up in Angel, so I assumed you did."

"I'm sure my mom was a wonderful person," Tate said. "I don't really know anything, though. What was her name?"

Jett's heart sank. "You don't know your mother's name?"

Tate smiled wryly. "You gotta remember, I thought I was an orphaned baby left on a doorstep until a few days ago. I know that Dr. Emmett is related to the Kings, of course, but I didn't run into them much so I don't know anything about them."

"Maddie," he said softly. "Her name was Maddie. She was one of the Jamisons, and her cousins were the Mitchells, so if you know any you're related to them. We both were related to the Emmetts, so the doctor is actually your uncle and your cousin."

A smile crept across the boy's face. "I guess I have a family tree now," he said. "Thomas King. That's a good name, don't you think? The son of Jett and Maddie King. Best looking family on the block." A sudden look of concern crossed his face. "I don't even know who I'm related to anymore. You gotta tell me, are we related to the Millers?"

Jett shook his head. "No, but I know them. Charlotte is around your age, isn't she?"

"Sixteen days younger," Tate mumbled. "You know what, I think they want to move me now. You'd better go talk to Anton."

A look of amusement crossed Jett's face. "You know what, I think I want to hear more about Charlotte Miller."

"She wants to be a nurse," Tate mumbled into his sheets. "She's a good girl, and Dr. Emmett really likes her, and… I'm not talking to you about this! Get out of here."

Jett laughed, standing up. "I think I'll go check on Anton now," he said. "Dr. Moon, take good care of Tate for me."

"I'll make sure he does," Dr. Emmett said.

"Hey," Tate said, halting Jett's progress. "...That's a pretty name, yeah? Maddie. Maddie, Jett and Thomas King."

"And Logan," Jett added. "You've got a little brother. He was born first, actually, but thanks to time-travel he's a lot younger than you."

"It's been kinda rough, you know?" said Tate. "Being adopted, having a voice in my head, and all that. Going to the 23rd century hasn't been a walk in the park either. But I think finding out who I really am makes it all worth it."

Jett's eyes watered and he blinked frantically. "I'm glad you think so," he said. He smiled at him and walked out.

He approached the room Valentine had given Anton. He rapped his knuckles against the door and waited. It only took a second for it to swing open.

"Yes sir?" Anton asked.

It was strange how Tate only looked like Maddie if Jett thought about it, while Anton always looked like a walking copy of her. He blinked the thought away.

"Can I come in?" he asked. "There's a few things I'd like to talk to you about."

Anton gripped the doorknob tighter but forced a smile. "Of course," he said through his teeth. Jett stepped in, feeling like an intruder, and the boy shut the door. The first thing Jett noticed was his jacket, folded neatly and set in the corner, and his face lit up.

Anton saw his expression and followed his gaze to make the connection. "Do you... do you want it back?" he faltered.

Jett wasn't sure of why Anton would care about it so much, but he was powerless to do anything against the boy's puppy eyes. "You can keep it," he said hastily. "I really don't need it. Valentine keeps the thermostat up in here."

"Zank you," he said softly. He pointed at an elaborately colored and embroidered futon with an array of fur blankets. "Would you like to sit down?"

Wondering why Valentine - or anyone - would have such a ridiculous piece of furniture, he sat down. Once he was seated, Anton cautiously took the other end of the futon, leaving a good deal of space between them. He then folded his hands and tilted his head in a clear display of deference, waiting for Jett to speak first.

Jett cleared his throat. "Well," he began, "For starters, I'd like to know if you're alright."

"I am fine, sir."

"Okay, good. Next, I'd like to know why I had to save you from the fire on Rendova."

The boy winced. "I am sorry, sir. I was not zinking."

"I'm not angry with you," Jett said. "You scared me, that's all."

"I have never seen anyzing like zat fire before. I know I shouldn't have, but I just wanted to see it," Anton said, getting nervous and starting to babble. "I know I am too curious, and I promise I will stop looking at zings and making you worry. I will never do it again, sir."

"Please don't call me sir," Jett said. "And it's okay to be curious, I just don't want you to die. Did Johnson let you run into danger like that?"

Anton shook his head. "It makes him very angry. But I can't help it sometimes. I will try to stop and not die."

"Okay, well, now that you're trying not to die let's move on," Jett said. "Do you know where Johnson is?"

Anton shook his head. "I do not know."

"Do you know how the *Kenswick* crashed?" he asked. "I can't imagine Johnson coming up with an escape plan that leaves you behind."

"He is a bad man, sir," Anton said, lifting his head for the first time. "He didn't tell me anyzing about an escape plan. I suppose it was his plan to leave me behind."

"Really?" Jett asked, uncertain. "I thought you were mutually attached to each other."

"I never want to see him again," Anton said vehemently.

Jett stared at him, rendered speechless by his son's outburst. His gaze slowly shifted from one of shock to thoughtfulness. "Tate said you were going to lie to me."

Anton's eyes widened. "Sir!"

"He didn't say what about, exactly. Just that he knew you were going to," Jett said. "But I want to believe you, I really do. Can I ask you one more thing?"

He nodded.

"Where's Johnson's time-travel watch?"

He watched the boy carefully, looking for nervousness or guilt, but the boy stared back unflinchingly. "I do not know," he said. "Mr. Johnson would never give it to me."

Jett rubbed his chin. "I'm going to try to believe you, Anton. If I tell you something, can you try to believe me?"

The boy hesitated, then nodded.

"Your mom would have loved you," Jett said simply, "But since she's gone I guess I'll try loving you enough for both of us. I'm sorry we weren't there for you, and I'm sorry Teddy Johnson did what he did. I really do want to make things right."

"I will try to believe you," Anton said. "Perhaps honesty runs in ze family?"

"Let's hope so, for both our sakes," Jett said.

18

Betrayal

That night, Anton lay awake. Valentine and his wife had provided dinner, and then everyone had gone to bed early. The window was open, letting in an occasional gust of salty air and the sound of the city trains whooshing along their tracks.

Something vibrated and he lurched out of bed and darted across the room. He fumbled with Jett's jacket, and pulled out Johnson's watch. The screen showed an incoming call. He bit his lip, but then took a chance and answered it.

"Hello?" he whispered, mindful of Jett in the other room. "Who are you?"

"Myshka!" a familiar voice breathed. Anton's hand shot up to smother his gasp.

"Mr. Johnson!" he whispered, trembling in excitement. "Are you still free?"

"Yes, and I talked to the SA president," he answered. "It's kind of his fault Duke came after us and destroyed Reka, but he's willing to clear my name and get us out of the city. I think it's safe for you to join me now. Where are you?"

"I am not sure. A man named Valentine took me and I am at his house. All ze people who were on ze *Starlight* are here, too."

There was a brief pause. "I need you to be very careful, then," said Johnson. "You can't let them notice you're leaving. Valentine's house is on the north end of 3rd street. I need you to find the train station on the south end. I have a friend who will meet you there and bring you to me."

Anton grabbed Jett's jacket and shrugged it on. "How will I know it's your friend?"

"I'll tell him to call you Myshka," Johnson decided. "Look here, boy; you trust me, don't you?"

"Of course, sir."

"Good. I've missed you. Wait five minutes, and then head out. See you soon."

Anton's face warmed with a smile. "See you soon."

The next five minutes were the slowest in his life. He sat on the futon, watching the seconds tick by. When the time was up, he laced up his boots and slipped out. Once on the street, he studied the signs and made his way to the south end.

The train station was in sight when his connection to Tate suddenly roared to life, as if his twin had just startled awake. His thoughts were clearer than Anton had ever heard them.

Anton, where are you?

"Tate?" he hissed.

Where are you? Can you hear me? Shouldn't you be asleep?

"I can take care of myself."

You're not looking for Johnson, are you? Tate sounded

alarmed. *Don't, Anton. The authorities will catch you before you get close to finding him.*

"I already found him," said Anton, letting the triumph leak into his voice. "It is too late for you to do anyzing. I am about to meet up wif him and zen I will be gone. Enjoy your time in Nebraska."

Johnson has literally killed people before! You can't go with him! He's not just evil, Anton, he's twisted. Turn around, now!

Ignoring him, Anton plowed on. Tate's voice in his head grew frantic as he approached the station, but it also grew quieter and soon it faded into nothing. Anton stepped onto the deserted platform and waited as a train whooshed in, its headlights slicing through the dark. A single passenger stepped out. The shadowy form in a dark suit stepped into the light of the station, and Anton froze.

"Mr. Duke?" he stuttered.

The man's eyes burned. He ran his fingers through his hair, fidgeting. "Myshka," he greeted.

Anton's eyes widened, but Johnson's voice was ringing in his head. *Look here, boy; you trust me, don't you?* It all made some kind of twisted sense, if Channyng was helping them out of the city and Duke was Channyng's assistant. Anton followed him onto the train and it swept them away. Neither of them spoke again.

When they got out, they were on the station in front of the SA complex. It was dark and drizzling slightly, so stepping into the lobby was a welcome change. It was almost as dark inside as out, however, since the lights turned off automatically this late at night. As they walked down the hallway, built-in sensors picked up their movements and the lights ahead of them flickered on, and the ones behind them shut off once they had passed. Thus they were accompanied by a consistent circle of light as they made their way to the second floor and to Channyng's office.

Teddy Johnson was pacing the room, while Channyng was flipping through a book. The moment the door swung open, Johnson rushed across the room, grabbing Anton by the shoulders and looking him up and down. "You're all right," he breathed. "Boy, I'm never letting you out of my sight again."

Behind them, Duke held the door open as several Security officers filed in. Anton hadn't seen them on his way in, so they must have been hiding in the hallway or an adjacent room. There were five of them, dressed for duty with their guns in their hands. Duke shut the door behind them with a finality that made Anton's heart sink. Johnson's face wrinkled and he stepped back. "What's this?" he demanded.

"This is you, under arrest," Channyng said, tossing the book aside as he stood up. He walked around the desk, smiling at the carpet before looking up. "The thing is, I don't need you, Teddy. You were useful on Reka for a while but after the mess you caused with the famine, and your obvious use of time-travel, it's just not worth keeping you around."

"You said you could clear my name!"

Channyng shrugged. "I could. But why would I? Maybe you didn't hear me the first time, but *I don't need you.* Anton, however..." his eyes trailed over to the boy.

Johnson lunged at Channyng, but the Security officers caught and restrained him. "You slinking, no-good, double-crosser!" Johnson raged, struggling to break free. "You'd use me as bait to catch Anton? I knew you were an entitled tyrant, but I thought actions like this were surely below you! And you!" He swung towards Duke. "You're handing us over to the Agency! I knew you weren't on my side, but I thought you'd at least be on Jesse King's!"

A sudden knocking put a stop to his rant. Everybody paused, looking at one another with varying degrees of confusion. Even Channyng looked a little nonplussed. One of the officers shuffled over to the door, standing on tip-toes to see out of the peephole. "Sir," he said, baffled, "it's the Head of Agriculture. Dr. Tyler-Duke!"

"Why is she here, Brandon?" Channyng demanded. "It's the middle of the night."

Duke looked just as confused as the rest of them. "I... I don't know," he stammered. "I'm her least favorite person. She's not looking for me!"

"Get her out of here. Officers, keep Johnson quiet until she's gone."

After a moment of hesitation, Duke steeled his nerves and opened the door just wide enough to slip through, closing it quickly. Sure enough, his mother was in the hallway, clutching her clipboard to her chest. Her hair was a frizzled mess and one of her socks was clearly showing between the top of her boot and the bottom of her skirt, while the other one had fallen down out of sight. Duke forced a smile, leaned against the door and folded his arms.

"You're up late," he said through his teeth.

She nodded, gazing into the middle distance. "Believe it or not, I've been looking for you."

"Mother, isn't your presentation tomorrow?" he asked, rubbing his eyes. "You should be getting a good night's sleep."

"Tomorrow is the most important day of my academic career," she said. "I couldn't sleep if I tried. I have spent years trying to find a way to terraform Mars. I have made it my life's work!"

"Then don't sleep," he said. "But you really need to go home."

"So do you," she snapped. "Why are you in Channyng's office this late at night? What kind of backstreet business are you getting yourself involved in? Why is it always politics instead of science with you! I bet your father is rolling over in his grave right now!" She stopped and sighed, her shoulders drooping. "I came looking for you to tell you something, and as usual you managed to make me lose my temper right off the bat."

"I didn't *make* you lose your temper," he said moodily. "That's kind of a personal problem."

She tilted her chin up, glaring at him. "Brandon, you're a bigger disappointment to me than I know what to do with. I came to ask for your help tomorrow, but I can tell that helping your mother is not something you'd be interested in."

She turned to leave, but Duke caught her arm. "You want my help?" he asked, dumbfounded.

"I *did*," she snapped, "for one weak, sentimental, misguided moment!"

"What do you want my help for?"

She made a frustrated noise. "The presentation, Einstein. I know it's been a while since you worked for me in Agriculture, but I thought you could remember enough to be my PA for the day instead of Channyng's. It's a big day for me, and I thought that if I had my son there… goodness, what am I saying? I can't ask for your help. It's demeaning for both of us."

"No, it's okay," he said. "I can see why it won't work. It's not demeaning for me, but it is for you. You're a renowned scientist and you're passionate about what you do. I'm the PA to a man that everyone knows is here for the power. Me publicly supporting you would be more embarrassing than anything."

"That is the position we're in, unfortunately," she said, and she actually looked sorry.

Duke's eyes simmered. "I think I get it now. Ever since the space station exploded, it's been an open secret that there's something wrong with me, and to a scientist of your renown, what would it do to your reputation if you were seen with me?"

The wrinkles around her eyes crinkled up in a glare. "I risked my reputation trying to be there for you after your father died, but you were too angry to let me! That's what tore us apart, Brandon. Don't pin this on me!"

"No, it's okay, mother," he said scathingly. "If I were you, I wouldn't want my good-for-nothing son around dirtying my shiny reputation either."

"It's not about my reputation!"

"Then prove it!"

She stomped her foot. "Come to the presentation with me tomorrow as my PA. It's one of the few times cameras will be allowed inside the complex, so if that doesn't prove I care more about you than my reputation I don't know what will!"

Duke stared at her, startled. There were no words to describe the intertwining hope and dread that he felt.

"I can't go. You don't want me there," he said at length. "I'm involved in worse things than you even realize."

"I'm your mother. If anybody can want you at your worst, it's me," she challenged. "Brandon, you're only proving me right. It's not me that ruined this relationship, it's you."

"Fine!" he snapped. "I'll be there! But don't be surprised if I get up to my usual backstreet business!"

"Well, don't think I hate you if I yell at you for it!"

"Goodnight!" he said angrily, turning away.

"Goodnight!" she shouted back, just as angrily, before storming down the hallway.

Duke pushed open the door and slammed it shut behind him. Channyng was sitting on his desk, looking at his book again, but he put it down as he came in. "Well?" he asked.

"She's gone," Duke said wearily.

"What did she want?"

Duke hesitated, but then shook his head. "I'd rather not say, sir."

Channyng raised a brow, but he let the matter drop. "Officers, you know what to do with Johnson. I want him confined here in the complex, but not anywhere that he or his guards will interfere with tomorrow's events. I want Anton here in my office with a constant guard until I have a chance to deal with him. You can get him water but nothing else: no visitors, no stepping outside this room. Duke, with me."

He grabbed his coat and strolled out of the room, and Duke followed him. They walked all the way downstairs to the front lobby before Channyng spoke.

"Duke, I'm worried about you."

Duke blinked. "Why?"

Channyng sighed, sitting on the edge of the reception desk. "Whose side are you really on? Ever since Reka, you've been a little wishy-washy. I want to be able to trust you but you make it so hard sometimes."

"I'm on your side, I swear. I brought you Anton. I'm practically betraying Jett and his friends just by being here right now. What else do I have to do to prove myself?"

The President sighed. "You need to stay away from your mom. I hate that it has to be this way, but she's never liked me. You can't be a good assistant to me and try to fix your relationship with her at the same time. Think about it this way. Everyone that matters in this city has their own agenda, whether it be scientific discovery like your mother or fame and recognition like Valentine. You can only pick one side."

"Well, I never picked your side. I just ended up here," Duke said.

Channyng gave a sympathetic smile. "I know, buddy. But I for one am glad things turned out this way, because in this game of agendas, you're a valuable asset. Whoever's side you're on is gonna win."

"Because I can time-travel," he guessed, tiredly.

"It's not even about that," Channyng said. "You're the best

of all of us. You're passionate like your mom, you're more likeable than Valentine any day, and you're smarter than Moon and Simons and all the rest of them. And I'd like to think I've taught you a thing or two about leadership in the ten years we've worked together."

Duke ran his fingers through his hair. "You killed Dr. Simons, didn't you? Have you been killing people behind my back for ten years?"

Channyng sighed. "I do it to protect you. Simons was asking too many questions."

"So we can just kill people whenever we feel like it?"

"We can," Channyng said earnestly.

"What if I don't want to? What if I want to live in a world where I can look my friends in the eye? A world where I can hug my mother without feeling blood on my hands?"

Channyng scooted off the desk and walked up to Duke. "Listen," he said softly, "forget all of that and think, just think for a moment. You and I are gonna go so far, you won't believe it. Our friends and family don't need us, and we don't need them. No more bothering with the little people. Now that we've got King and Anton, we can find Angel's Crypt. After that, we won't be the two most powerful people in Nova Atlantis anymore. We're gonna be the two most powerful people in all of time and space."

Duke's flickering eyes met Channyng's. "You and I, huh?"

Channyng grinned. "You know it."

"Even without time-travel... I'm powerful?"

The man's smile grew. "More than anyone."

Duke dropped his head, hiding his smile. "Okay," he said. "Okay. See you tomorrow, sir."

19

Debts Paid

Morning dawned, and Johnson was pacing his eight by eight foot cell. Gears inside of the door began to turn and click and it ground open, and Johnson stopped his pacing. He squinted as bright light from the hallway streamed in, like a flashlight shining in his eyes. "You may close ze door. I will speak wif him alone," he heard a familiar voice say, and the speaker stepped into the light and into the room. The inner workings of the door started grinding again, sliding the high-security door shut with a *clang*.

As the light faded away, Johnson was left alone in his cell with Ivan Koswitch.

"President Johnson," Ivan said with exaggerated reverence, touching his forehead in the traditional greeting. "I hope you are well?"

"Skip the mockery," Johnson growled. He grabbed Ivan by the shoulders, slamming him against the wall. "Where have you been?"

"I have been saving your neck, Sur Liedr," he said placidly, unconcerned with being pinned. "You would have never escaped ze *Kenswick* wifout me. I have no great love for the Space Agency and I have no problem sabotaging zeir work."

Johnson's eyes widened. "You were behind the *Kenswick's* crash?"

"Hush!" Ivan snapped. "Recording equipment may not be allowed, but zat doesn't mean zere is nobody listening. Zere is only one zing I want more zan to return to my own country, and zat is ze destruction of zis city. President Channyng has played wif all of us."

"I'll help you," Johnson said eagerly. He let go of the man to resume his pacing. "I know we've had our differences, but this is something I can get behind. Get me out of here and I swear I'll burn this city to the ground!"

Ivan eyed him coolly. "If you want me to get you out, you know what, or rather, *who*, you must give me."

Johnson froze. "You... you can't be serious," he said. "Look here, if you think you can blackmail me into giving you Anton like this..."

"Zat is my offer, take it or leave it," Ivan said, raising his voice to interrupt. "And I will not stand for any double-crossing on your part. Look at us now, Johnson. I have ze upper hand in all zings - money, position, power, freedom. You are in, as my people would say, ze *prey position*."

"You no-good, slimy, heartless scoundrel!" Johnson shouted. He punched the door in his rage. "You're taking away the last thing I cared about. Take the boy, but may you wallow in your guilt like the wretch you are! And listen, Ivan Koswitch: I get the watch."

"You may have ze watch," Ivan said with a little nod of

acquiescence. The locking mechanisms in the door began to whir and the door began to open. "I will arrange for you to have ze watch and transportation out of ze city. I have already arranged a plan for tonight zat will bring ze SA to its knees. After zat, ze boy goes wif me and you and I will benefit from some time apart." He stepped out into the light. As the door began to close, he glanced over his shoulder. "So you know, President Johnson: I consider your debts paid."

The door clanged shut.

That same morning, at the Valentines' home, Jett walked into the dining room to find Parker and Robbie at the table. It was a massive oak table, with twelve intricately carved matching chairs.

"Have we heard anything from Dr. Emmett?" Jett asked, sitting beside them.

Parker shook her head. "No," she answered. "I haven't seen the Valentines all morning, either. The house is empty besides us. Oh, and Anton, but I guess he's still sleeping."

Jett frowned. "Valentine just left us here?"

As if on cue, the front door opened. Valentine swaggered in, and to everyone's surprise he was followed by Cariss.

"This woman says she knows you," Valentine said with a dramatic shrug.

Cariss got straight to the point. "All of you need to leave this city right away. Duke intends to hand you over to Channyng, whether you're willing or not."

Parker gasped and Robbie's face fell.

Jett jumped up, nearly knocking over his chair. "I've been saying this whole time that we should be back in Nebraska already," he said. "Let's go. Where's Anton?"

"At the complex," Cariss said, stopping him in his tracks. "Channyng and Duke somehow managed to lure him out. They've also secured Johnson, who is headed for prison, while I believe Anton is in Channyng's personal custody."

"Where is Duke?" Parker demanded. A storm was brewing on her face.

Cariss shrugged. "Yesterday, he left me at his house. I haven't seen him since, even though I've been looking."

"I don't have time for this," Valentine interrupted. "I'm supposed to be at the complex right now, hosting a press conference. As much as I hate to lose my chance at Angel's Crypt, I can take all of you back to the *Starlight* if we leave right away."

"I'm not leaving without Anton," Jett said firmly. "Where are they keeping him?"

"I'd guess he's at the SA complex," Valentine said. "But the place is swarming with people. There's a demonstration tonight for Agriculture in hopes of getting more government funding. There are ambassadors from countries all over the world coming, so Security will be tripled."

"The more people there are, the easier to blend in," Jett reasoned.

"Jett, that's crazy!" Robbie said. "You're gonna walk into the complex in broad daylight and drag him out?"

"He might refuse to go with you," Cariss said. "He has a better chance at being reunited with Johnson by staying here than by coming with us."

"So we kidnap him," Parker said.

Robbie sank back in his chair. "You're as crazy as Jett is."

"If you think you can take Anton from Channyng, you're mistaken," Valentine said with a short laugh of disbelief. "He has this entire city under his thumb. And even without that, you don't know your way around the complex. It's a black-tie event, and you'd need to know how to act."

Jett looked at him meaningfully. "We might need a guide."

Valentine looked horrified. "There's no way I'm helping you."

Jett glanced at Parker. She was twitching with pent-up frustration, glaring daggers at Valentine. Jett took a deep breath, schooling his features into a taunting smile. "Then there's no way I'll ever even *consider* sharing Angel's Crypt with you once I find it," he said. He shook his head at the man's blank look. "You're not the only one who knows more than they're letting on. Someone left a riddle for me on Rendova, so I'm guessing the person who hid it wants me to be the one to find it. I'm leaps and bounds ahead of you. There's no way you'll ever find it without me."

"Someone… left you a riddle?" Valentine stuttered. For the first time since they'd known him, his smile had failed and he could hardly string two words together. "You're… *you're* going to find it?"

Parker's face broke into a lopsided smile. "Yes, we're gonna find it," she joined in. "It's practically ours already. So are you gonna help us or not?"

"Okay, okay, let me think." Valentine pulled at his tie and the gears of his mind turned. "First of all, I need to see if Julia can come back and get you dressed appropriately."

"The four of us need to get inside," Jett said. "Me, Parker, Robbie and Cariss."

"But we need an escape plan for all of you plus Tate and Dr. Emmett, because once Channyng knows what's going on it's gonna be a reign of terror." Valentine swaggered towards the door, pushing his hands into his pockets. "I need to talk to Julia and see how things are going at the complex. I'll come up with something, no worries!"

Once he was gone, Robbie tentatively moved his arm and winced. "I'm gonna look funny at a black-tie event with my arm in a sling."

"It won't be unusual. The people around here are always getting themselves injured," Cariss said dismissively.

Robbie tilted his head. "Really? Why?"

"A good deal of them are scientists conducting highly dangerous experiments. Not to mention the assassination attempts."

"Lovely. What a lovely place to live!" Robbie groaned.

Parker gave Jett a lopsided smile. "I hope Valentine doesn't see through your bluff about Angel's Crypt."

"I wasn't bluffing," he argued.

She snorted. "I thought you didn't want to get involved. And anyway, we don't know the poem."

"Ah. About that." Jett reached into his pocket and pulled out a piece of paper. He tried looking nonchalant as he handed it over, but his insides were churning. He had spent a good portion of the night with pen and paper in anticipation of this moment.

With a frown, Parker took the paper, unfolding it and smoothing out the edges. Her eyes darted over the light sketch, and Jett could tell by the way her face lit up the exact moment she realized what it was. "Jesse, did you… is this a sketch of Rendova beach?"

He shrugged. "Sure, but you're looking on the wrong side."

She flipped it over and gasped as she scanned the words. "The poem! You remembered it!"

"Sure," he shrugged again. "I'm good at that kind of thing."

"You're amazing, Jesse King," she said passionately. "Forget whatever I said before. Thank you, thank you, thank you!"

She gave him a brief hug before looking at the paper again. "You're a good artist," she said admiringly. "I could never sketch something like this."

"We can talk art later," Jett promised, "but right now we need to come up with a plan. This is going to be difficult without Duke."

"He's gotta be on our side still," Robbie said, shaking his head. "We just need to talk with him. I still trust him."

"People change," Jett said.

"And we didn't know him that well in the first place," Parker added. "We're going to have to find a way to work without him, possibly against him."

"Duke is an extremely loyal man," Cariss said. "Unfortunately his loyalty has been toward Channyng for longer than he's known you, even longer than he's known me. I don't believe he wishes any real harm on any of you, he's simply confused about who's side he's on. I do know that he considered you to be his friends."

"How long have you known him?" Parker asked.

"Nearly ten years," she shrugged.

Jett frowned. "Are you from my century or his?"

"Yours, but I met Duke long before he ever started looking for you and Johnson. I was the first person to time-travel with him. He showed me this city, and I have actually spent a lot of my time here."

Parker wrinkled her nose. "Why?"

"I see a problem and I want to fix it," Cariss said. Though she was as bland as usual, Jett noticed an unusual strength in the way she spoke. "This city is against life, freedom, and a host of other things, so it needs to end. I am part of an undercover movement to do just that."

Robbie's eyes widened. "That is definitely not what I was expecting. Does Duke know?"

She shook her head. "Unfortunately he isn't ready to know," she said. "I hope that someday he'll join the movement as well, but right now he doesn't know of its existence."

"How do you get rid of a city?" Jett asked.

"It takes a lot of anonymous essays, for starters," she said. "We want to change the public opinion of Nova Atlantis from something good to something bad. We also find ways to collect evidence of the atrocities that happen here. Almost everything is legal in this city, and we want to show the public the terrible things that the people here do."

"If Duke doesn't even know about this movement, it can't be that influential," Parker said.

"It's bigger than you might think. As you can imagine, anybody who dares to question this city is quickly silenced, whether by being kicked out or killed. Because of that, the movement is top secret. Most of the people in it don't know the real identities of the others."

"So anybody around us could be part of this movement," Jett said thoughtfully.

The front door opened and Julia bustled in, wearing her usual Security uniform. "Good morning everyone," she greeted cheerfully. "I'm sorry I disappeared. Ernest and I are both very, very busy today! He's doing a press conference right now. In fact, it's probably on the TV."

She turned it on and sure enough, Valentine was on the screen. The press conference was taking place outside of the SA complex, in a large, outdoor pavilion. The pavilion was full of reporters, snapping pictures and struggling to get close to the stage. Valentine stood behind a podium, answering a question about the Space Agency's ten year plan to terraform Mars.

"He's so good at what he does," Julia said with a happy sigh.

Jett frowned at the TV. Valentine's publicity smile made him look like a grinning shark. His hands were in his pockets, and the way he stood shouted arrogance. He did have charisma, though. He flattered the reporters, entertained the crowd with humor, and praised the people he worked with, painting them out to be the loveliest people on the planet.

"Do you mind if I leave this on?" Julia asked them. "I'd like to keep an eye on how the conference is going."

"It's fine," Jett assured her.

"Sweet. Now, let's take a look at you guys." She rubbed her hands together, looking at them with a wide grin. "This is gonna be so much fun!"

And so it began. Julia swept around her house, finding clothes and accessories to get them what she called 'properly dressed.' Jett was given a suit to put on, and he had a nagging suspicion that it cost as much money as he made in a year. He felt a little ridiculous but at least it fit him.

Julia turned the dining room into some kind of a salon, putting Parker's hair into an extravagant updo and giving Jett an impromptu haircut, right then and there. Cariss refused any help from anybody, and dressed in a black suit and painted her nails to match. Robbie, however, needed a lot of help, from doing his hair to tying his tie.

Julia dragged a mirror into the room, encouraging them to look at themselves. When Jett looked in it, he saw a pampered young man with far too much hair gel, dressed in a three piece suit and tie. The image was far removed from the small-town Nebraskan he really was. The full weight of what he was about to do dawned on him, and his heart stuttered a little. Maybe he'd fit in at the event with his outward appearance, but he knew better than anyone the small, ordinary man he was on the inside.

Julia bit her tongue, carefully applying Parker's makeup. "You're going to go in with Dr. Moon," she explained. "He'll be here to pick you up soon. He knows how to act, so act like he does."

"Why aren't you going?" Parker asked.

She laughed. "I don't like to show my face in public. But I'll be there, hiding in a shadow somewhere."

"Will the press conference be over before we get there?" Jett asked, watching the TV.

Julia nodded. "It's almost over. Once it ends, the more distinguished guests will arrive and the presentation will take place inside the complex, along with a fancy dinner."

On the TV, Valentine droned on with glorious descriptions

of the SA. "We're a team," he was saying, "we're more than that, we're a family. We work together and we dream together. We look at the stars and we say, 'you know what? We can get there. We can go farther.' There is nowhere I'd rather be than right here in Nova Atlantis, helping people fulfill their dreams, and getting the help to fulfill mine."

Jett shook his head. "It's all nonsense! He himself has said that everyone wants to kill each other here."

Julia giggled. "He's a good liar, isn't he?"

"So it's all lies?" Jett pressed, and some nagging thought inside of him felt validated. "He doesn't believe a word he's saying, does he?"

Julia straightened nervously, turning to fix Robbie's hair. "I didn't mean that. He loves Nova Atlantis."

"Does he?" Jett pushed. "I can't say that I like him, but he doesn't seem as evil as everyone else. It's almost like he says all these lies to cover up why he's really here."

"I don't know what you mean," she said.

"Is Valentine part of the secret movement to shut down Nova Atlantis?" he asked.

She backed away like he'd released a bomb. "That's ridiculous."

Jett sighed. "I guess I shouldn't ask. If he is, I understand why you need to keep it a secret. But I've seen the future now, and it worries me. If a man like Valentine was part of an organization to make things right, that's one thing that might give me hope."

Julia fiddled with the brush in her hand. "I shouldn't tell you this, but I will. You're absolutely right. He's the leader of the movement. He's determined to be the man who puts an end to Nova Atlantis."

Parker looked shocked. "I assumed he was only here for the power."

Julia laughed, shaking her head. "People assume a lot of things about him," she said fondly. "Hardly any of it is true. He and Moon pretend to be bitter enemies so that if one of them ever gets accused of undermining this city, the other one will most likely be safe."

"So Dr. Moon is part of the movement, too," Jett said.

She nodded. "His right hand man."

"Guys, look at the screen!" Parker said. "Look, look, look!"

Valentine was still onscreen, along with a handful of people waiting at the edge of the stage. "No more questions for today," he was saying. "We're almost done here, but I'd like the Head of Agriculture to say a few words. Our plans for Mars begin with this amazing woman here. Make welcome Dr. Tyler-Duke!"

Dr. Tyler-Duke stepped up to the podium, and Jett saw why Parker was so excited. Duke was standing behind her. The woman handed her clipboard to him, and he stood in the background holding it for her while she gave a short speech.

"Dr. Tyler-Duke? Is that his mother?" Jett asked.

Robbie frowned. "He has a mother?"

"Of course he does," Parker said. "The real question is, what's his actual name? Don't tell me it's Duke Tyler-Duke!"

"His name is Brandon. Duke is merely his nickname," Cariss said. "And yes, that's his mother."

"But he's standing where her PA is supposed to stand!" Julia gasped. "Did Channyng approve this?"

"Channyng would never approve of something like this," Cariss said drily. "Duke seems to have grown a will of his own. Miracle of miracles."

The door opened and Dr. Moon stepped in. "Come see this!" Julia said. "Look, Duke is acting as his mother's PA!"

Moon glanced at the TV. "I know," he said. "He's been following her around all day; everyone is talking about it. Is everyone ready? The guests are starting to arrive, so I think it's high time I bring you over there."

"We're ready," Jett said.

"Good. By the way, I looked around and found that Anton is being kept in Channyng's office," Moon said.

"Channyng will be down at the presentation, though, so he shouldn't get in the way," said Julia.

"There are two Security officers guarding Anton," Dr. Moon said. "If we can distract them, you're pretty much home free. There will be too much going on for Channyng to notice that anything's amiss. All right, everyone, we need to take our leave. Tate and Dr. Emmett are already waiting in the *Starlight*."

"Wait a moment!" Julia complained. She was desperately trying to brush Robbie's hair into shape.

Parker clunked across the floor, still getting used to her heels, and she followed Dr. Moon out the door. Cariss was close behind. Robbie tied his laces and then bolted to catch up with them, and Julia chased him, still working on his hair. "Ma'am, I'm sure it's fine," Robbie said, ducking away from her and out the door.

Jett gave her a wry smile. "Thanks for everything," he said. "I hope none of you get in trouble for helping us."

She smiled, patting his arm. "It's a risk we're willing to take."

Jett stepped outside. "I'm glad to see our future is in such safe hands," he said.

The last thing he saw before closing the door was Julia's peaceful smile. The warmth of the Valentine home was shut away behind an extravagant oak door, leaving him out in the drizzling cold.

The others were already halfway to the station. Jett could see the blue skyscrapers looming in the distance, like castles of ice in a wintry world. A chilling wind breathed against him and he reached to pull his jacket tighter, but instead he felt the cashmere suit he was wearing. Holding back a shiver, he squared his shoulders and stepped onto the street.

20

The Presentation

They got to the station right as a train whooshed in, and Valentine jumped out of it. "I slipped away during Dr. Tyler-Duke's speech," he said. "I always say five minutes, and she always takes twenty. Officially, the conference is over, but we still have to hurry. Everybody's going to wonder where I went." He hustled them into the waiting train. It was empty like the station, and Jett noticed for the first time that these trains didn't have drivers.

"All right, listen close," Valentine said once they were all seated. "Moon will get you seated at a table while I take a look around. Anton's still in the President's office, so I'm assuming Channyng means to leave him there until the event is over. Our only escape plan so far is all of you making a mad dash for the space dock, and you hopefully get out of here in that bucket of scraps."

"It's actually a 3000 model racer, best there ever was," Robbie muttered.

"Dr. Emmett and Tate are already there, right?" Valentine

asked, and Moon nodded so he continued. "As crazy as this plan sounds, I honestly don't think it should be too difficult. And Anton isn't legally a prisoner, so we're not breaking any laws in case anyone is worried about that, which I think would only be me."

"So you all know, I will not be going to the *Starlight*," Cariss announced. She had been so quiet, Jett had almost forgotten she was there. "I will assist you in any way possible, however."

"Why aren't you coming?" Parker asked. "We can't leave you behind. You're from the 21st century, same as us!"

"I intend to stay with Duke," she said calmly. "I have known him for much longer than any of you have, and I have been trying to convince him to leave this city. I won't leave until he does."

"We're here," Dr. Moon announced.

The complex was somehow bigger than Jett remembered. Two identical skyscrapers stood side by side, joined by a domed building on the ground with the pavilion behind it. It reminded him of the block towers he used to build with Logan; connected buildings sprawled over the bright green grass, all of them different sizes and shapes.

"Take this," Valentine instructed, pushing something into Jett's hand. "It's an earpiece designed to look like a hearing aid, so no one will question it. Julia got us the good stuff. Put this little mike under your collar where no one can see it. I've got a radio in my pocket, so I can hear everything around you and if necessary I can speak to you through the earpiece. Got it?"

"Got it," Jett said, working hard to keep his voice from shaking.

"Good. Everybody remember, if I'm not around King's the boss. If he gives an order, follow it."

They stepped onto the platform and followed the walkway into the complex. The doors swung open on their own accord, and Valentine led them down a maze of hallways with Moon bringing up the rear. They came to a set of double doors that were opened wide, with light and music tumbling out.

The room they entered was like nothing Jett had ever seen before. The trademark blue glass was gone, replaced with a vaulted ceiling and walls that were covered in thick curtains. Chandeliers were hung on intermittent beams, and violin music was coming from somewhere, though Jett was too dazzled to pinpoint where. There were round tables set up with white tablecloths, and each one had a small, recycling water fountain set up in the middle or some other kind of elaborate display.

It was a banquet hall, Jett's mind registered numbly. When he thought of the complex he had come to imagine labs and workshops and offices, not a display of money and useless elegance. The hall was crowded, and people ate and drank, dressed in suits and evening gowns.

At one end of the room was a wide contraption that to Jett looked like a mix between a table and a pool. It was made of metal and set up like a table, but instead of a flat top there was a dip of several inches that had been filled with water. Several people dressed in lab coats were bustling around it, most likely preparing the display of pseudo-fire.

His staring was interrupted when he heard Robbie behind him. "Are the heels necessary?" he was whispering to Parker, whom Moon had pushed onto his good arm. "I'm afraid you're gonna step on me. If you're really that short I can find you a stool."

Jett turned to ask Valentine what to do next, but to his dismay the man had vanished. He looked for Dr. Moon, but the man had wandered away and was deep in a conversation with one of the lab-coat people. He cast a pleading look at Cariss, who shrugged. "I was told you're the boss," she said simply.

Squaring his shoulders, Jett turned to face the room. "Let's find a table," he said, hoping Valentine would correct him through the radio in his ear if he did anything wrong. "There's an empty one over there. Come on."

He led the group to a table and they all took a seat. Instantly, a man in a white apron was there, serving some kind of appetizer and a bottle of wine. The moment he was gone, Jett heard Valentine's voice in the earpiece.

"When someone is talking to you, tilt your head towards them to give them the impression you're deaf. Also, good job so far. You have no obligation to speak to the servers; you can ignore an outright question if you want to. If you want to avoid strangers introducing themselves to you, keep up a steady conversation with the people at your table and don't look around."

Quickly he searched for something to say. His eye landed on the wall behind the display table and he saw a faint glimmer. "I think there's a screen hidden there," he said, turning to the others. "Right now it's just showing a wood paneled wall to blend in."

"I think I see it!" said Parker. "That's a huge screen. Maybe they're going to give a video presentation about the fire or something."

"What is this?" asked Robbie, poking at the plate of appetizers.

"I'm guessing it used to live in the ocean, but I really don't know," said Jett. "Do you think they cooked it?"

"Send Robbie toward the back of the hall," said Valentine in his ear. "I'm going to show him a couple different ways out."

"Robbie, Valentine needs you in the back," he said quietly, still pretending to investigate the food.

The pilot nodded, excusing himself and disappearing. A moment later, Dr. Moon joined them, taking an empty seat. "This whole event is silly," he declared, low and unimpressed. "I wouldn't fund this project for anything."

"What exactly is this event about?" asked Jett.

"They're hoping to get more funding from different governments in the Alliance. They want to use pseudo-fire to help terraform Mars. Something about melting the oceans and releasing oxygen into the atmosphere. I think it's ridiculous."

"Will it get any funding?"

Moon sighed. "Of course. Ambassadors love this kind of thing."

Robbie came back, sliding into his seat. "I saw the dish-room, guys," he said, his eyes as wide as saucers. "It's all automated. You could throw a dirty dish in there and the kitchen will clean it and put it on the shelf all on its own. It's amazing."

"Why does that surprise you? I thought you were from an even further point in the future," said Parker.

"That doesn't mean I'm familiar with every kind of technology. Where I grew up, we hung our clothes on clotheslines. I wasn't raised by robots or whatever you're thinking."

Suddenly the lights dimmed. Anybody left standing scrambled for a seat. Moon slipped away without explanation, leaving them on their own.

A man with dark almond eyes and a winning smile wearing a bespoke vicuña suit and crocodile leather shoes stepped to the front, holding a microphone. "Good evening, everyone," he greeted good-naturedly. "As you all know, my name is Channyng, and I've had the pleasure of working for the SA for fifteen years. I'm privileged to say that I've known Dr. Tyler-Duke for every one of those. I promise you, she is gonna blow you away with this presentation tonight."

Jett guessed that the reporters in the room had some kind of permit for taking pictures, since the flashing of their cameras was almost constant.

"Before we introduce her, however," Channyng continued, "I'd like to say a few words about Dr. Simons, one of the Heads here who died in an unfortunate accident earlier this week."

As he talked, the chair next to Jett squeaked as a late arrival pulled it out. "Greetings," the newcomer whispered, seating himself.

"Ivan?" Jett stared in disbelief, watching the Rekan settle down in the chair. Trying to keep his voice down, he hissed, "What on earth are you doing here?"

"I was in ze area, so I zought I'd stop by," Ivan answered. "I am a member of ze Space Agency, after all. I did not realize you were, zough. I zought you were from Nebraska?" He gave him a pointed look.

"You were Johnson's right hand man," Jett whispered back, desperately hoping that Valentine was listening. "I know nobody else suspects you, but I'm convinced you're involved in everything he did."

He shrugged. "As you say, nobody else suspects me. What do I have to worry about?"

He turned away to listen to Channyng. Jett fidgeted in his chair, resisting the urge to speak directly to Valentine and blow his cover. *Johnson is free, Johnson is free,* his mind crowed, repeating it like a mantra. Cariss believed that Johnson was in custody, but so had everyone when he was on the *Kenswick.* And even if Ivan was someone else's pawn, or here of his own volition, it didn't bode well. Jett pressed his lips together, trying to ignore the pounding of his heart. *Johnson is free, Johnson is free.*

21

Return of the Rekans

Channyng's eulogy to Dr. Simons was droning on in the banquet hall. Duke was in a room behind the stage, listening to the speech with one ear while the rest of his attention was devoted to his mother, who was rushing around her team, overseeing their work and checking her clipboard frantically. Several of her scientists were double checking special fire extinguishers; they held a special mixture that would put the fire out instantly if the situation called for it.

Duke caught his mother as she swept by, halting her abruptly. "You should sit down," he admonished. "We're ready, aren't we? Relax."

She sank against him, heaving a sigh. "I can't believe this day is finally here. Oh, I'm nothing but a bundle of nerves." She pulled away from him, clutching her clipboard. "I want to say, Brandon, that today… it's been nice. I'm not forgiving you for the past ten years," she added quickly, shaking a pen at him, "but I truly do appreciate your help today."

"Of course, mother," he said. He glanced toward the stage door and listened; Channyng was still talking. "Would you excuse me? There's something I need to check on. I'll be back to watch your presentation, I promise."

"Like you said, we really are done here," she said with a contented sigh, looking around the room. "Go ahead. I'll see you out there."

Duke nodded and ducked out a side exit. He was more than familiar with the layout of the complex, having grown up with parents who worked here and then working here himself for ten years. He navigated through out-of-the-way hallways, and stepped into an elevator and went up to the second floor. As he stepped out, he saw two Security officers standing guard over Channyng's office door.

He squared up, straightening his tie before swaggering towards them. "Good evening," he greeted nonchalantly. He reached for the door, but one of the officers stopped him.

"We... we... we have orders not to let anyone in," he stuttered, sheepishly.

Duke took a step back, studying the officer's face. "You look familiar. You were in the docking bay yesterday, weren't you?"

The officer nodded.

"Well, then, let's not repeat mistakes."

"Let him in," the other officer hissed. "This is Channyng's PA. He's allowed wherever he wants."

The officer stepped aside. Shooting him a thin smile, Duke pushed open the door.

He had to squint to make sense of the darkness. Anton was on Channyng's personal chair, and Duke saw the glint of handcuffs behind him, keeping him trapped in the chair. The

Security officer shut the door behind him, leaving the room lit only by the dim glow behind the window blinds.

Anton eyed him suspiciously, so Duke walked slowly, holding up his hands. "It's just me," he said.

"What do you want?" the boy asked, his voice hoarse.

"I don't want anything from you," Duke said, honestly, "Nothing I deserve, anyway." He glanced at the handcuffs. Taking a moment to dig through Channyng's desk, he found the key and knelt behind the chair. "I'm sorry about all this," he said. "Do you know where you want to go? I can get you back to Nebraska, or anywhere else you'd like."

"Zey are letting me go?"

"I am, yes." The handcuffs slid open and Duke pulled them off, dropping them onto the floor. "Not on Channyng's order, though. He looked ready to kill me when I helped my mother at the press conference, so goodness knows what he'll do after this."

"Zen why are you doing zis?"

He sighed and ran his fingers through his hair. "I'm trying to undo my mistakes. And because I owe your father. Don't think I'm a hero or anything."

Anton frowned. "You owe Jett King?"

"I owe him my life because I'm the one who's going to take away his. I can't ever make it up to him, or Cariss, or my mother, but I'd like to lessen their disappointment if that's still possible."

"I do not understand. You will be in trouble if you help me escape."

Duke walked over to the bookshelf, thumbing through the

volumes. "Maybe with Channyng. He might have me killed like he did Dr. Simons. Even if he lets me live, I'll definitely never get that job in Agriculture I want."

Anton stood, grabbed Jett's jacket off the desk and shrugged it on. "You should not do zis zen. I am not even on your side. If Mr. Johnson told me to kill you, I would."

"Aha." Duke pulled *Angel's Crypt: A Publication of the Riddles* off of the shelf. He tucked the small book in the inner pocket of his suit. "You know Anton, I was exactly like you yesterday. I was angry and betrayed and lonely. And if Channyng had told me to kill you, I would've done it. But that just makes us both fools, doesn't it?"

Anton's look was smoldering. "I am not a fool."

"You are if you think Johnson wouldn't stab you in the back if it helped his plans," Duke said. "I'm afraid I've bought into the lies of this city my entire life. But I'm giving them up, starting now. I don't want to be used. I want to do good. Be forgiven. Love my mother."

He headed towards the door, his dress shoes silent on the carpeted floor. Anton hurried to catch up. "Can't you love your mom wifout getting yourself killed? Am I supposed to come wif you? Won't zey stop us?"

"No one will stop us. I'm Channyng's PA, which I've been told makes me the second most powerful person in this city. But do you see my eyes?" They flickered hungrily as he pushed open the door. "I think that makes me number one."

The officers gaped in surprise as Duke strolled out, followed by Anton. "Keep guarding the office, please," Duke said. "Wouldn't want anyone wandering in." Both of them reached for their weapons, hesitated, and then slumped in defeat and confusion. They stayed at their posts.

Duke and Anton approached the elevator, but the metal doors opened unexpectedly. Valentine swaggered out, holding a radio to his ear, but he stumbled to a halt when he saw them. His eyes darkened. "Mr. Duke, step away from the kid. You and Channyng have no right to keep him here."

Duke stepped between him and Anton. "Channyng has nothing to do with this. You're the one who needs to step back. I'm not about to let you have him."

Valentine's eyes opened comically wide. "I think we misunderstand each other!" he said. "I'm here on behalf of Jett King."

"I'm here on behalf of Anton Venedict," Duke said drily. "So please, step out of the way."

Holding his hands up, Valentine scooted away from the elevator. "Jett is hoping to rescue Anton and then escape in the *Starlight*," he said. "He and his friends are down there, watching the presentation. You should talk to them. Preferably before Channyng notices anything and burns the place down looking for you two."

"We'll consider it," Duke said, stepping into the elevator. He pulled Anton in and the doors slid shut.

"I want to talk wif Jett King," Anton said abruptly.

Duke glanced at him. "You sure?"

The boy nodded, though his face was pale as a ghost.

They reached the bottom floor. As the elevator doors opened they heard Dr. Tyler-Duke's voice from the banquet hall, amplified by speakers, explaining the process they went through to invent water-burning fire. The two of them headed toward the big entrance doors that led into the banquet hall. A Security guard stood there idly, along with a few people who couldn't find a place to sit. Duke joined them, folding his arms and leaning against the doorway, and Anton hovered behind him.

The room was dark as spotlights pointed at the stage. Despite the dim lighting, Duke saw Parker sitting at a table near the center of the room, and if he squinted he thought he could make out Cariss. There were several more shadowy figures at the table, who he assumed were Jett and the rest of his friends. He looked over the other tables, idly picking out his coworkers: Dr. Moon was sitting with his family, the secretary was sitting in the back, the Head of Engineering was sitting near the front with his fiancée from Health and Safety, and there were numerous others that he knew. The rest of the crowd were journalists, ambassadors, politicians and science peers, along with the occasional Security officer.

Even from the doorway, Duke had a good view of the presentation. The wall behind the display table was indeed a screen, and it flickered to life with pie charts and diagrams. His mother was talking, looking as frazzled and passionate as usual. "We needed something that would keep its own current of something like magnesium and a metal oxide, as well as something that would stick to the hydrogen in water without being affected by the oxygen," she was saying. She gestured to the screen. "Thankfully, we found our answer."

She glanced at the crowd, and her face lit up when she saw Duke in the doorway. She continued her speech ardently.

Duke's eyes wandered over the display table. It was full of water and securely bolted to the floor. Clear, protective panels were set up along the edges. The fire hadn't been lit yet, so the water was placid and undisturbed.

Anton tugged on his suit. "Sir," he whispered, "Zere is somezing wrong."

Duke's eyes shot to the platform where his mother was still talking blissfully. "What is it?" he whispered back.

"I see several men from Weka," Anton said, struggling with his pronunciation of *Reka*. "Zey are Ivan Koswitch's closest friends and advisors. Zey are usually up to no good. Zey are standing in ze shadows, and I zink zey have pistols."

Duke studied the crowd again, and he made out at least five men milling around in the very back, not far from them, with haggard, bearded faces and hollow eyes. He saw the unmistakable glint of a laser pistol in one of their hands.

"Were they on the ship with you?" he asked.

Anton nodded. "I zink zey are ze ones who crashed ze *Kenswick*. Ze people of Weka do not like ze Space Agency. Whatever zey are up to, it is not good."

"Do you think they're working with Johnson?"

The boy hesitated. "I do not know," he said after a moment. "Mr. Johnson does not like zem, but he has had to work wif zem before."

The fire display had gotten to the interesting part. The Agriculture team crowded around the pool, finding their positions. "Ladies and gentlemen," Dr. Tyler-Duke said, her eyes glowing, "I present to you the latest achievement of science, and the fruit of our labor: the newly dubbed *Ardenti Aqua*."

Flames erupted on the surface of the water, safely contained but using the whole pool to dance and flit around. The crowd *oohed* and *ahhed* and reporters darted closer, clicking their cameras.

In the doorway, a man who was undoubtedly a Rekan began whispering to the small crowd of people. "Step in, please, we were told to close ze doors. Ze doors are closing, everyone."

Duke grabbed Anton and jerked him out of the room. The Rekan ushered everyone out of the doorway and further into the banquet hall, and then he shut the door, leaving Duke and Anton alone in the hallway. The lock clicked.

"The Rekans have everyone trapped in there," Duke said, pushing his hands through his hair. His face was as white as a sheet. "This isn't good. Come on, I know a back entrance to the stage."

22

Chaos

Jett was getting anxious. It had been several minutes since he'd last heard from Valentine, and Ivan Koswitch was still sitting next to him, twirling his beard and nodding his head, seemingly fully interested in the presentation.

At long last his earpiece buzzed. "We might have to have a change of plans," Valentine said. "Duke has Anton, and I don't know where they went."

A thousand questions swirled in Jett's brain, but it was impossible to ask any of them. He sat there, fidgeting, hoping Valentine would say more.

After a few moments he did. "All right, another plot twist. I'm trying to get into the banquet hall but I can't. The doors are locked, which was definitely not supposed to happen."

Jett rubbed his jaw, hoping it wasn't obvious that he was having a mental breakdown. He counted the seconds until Valentine spoke again.

"So, you're all locked in the banquet hall. Is everything going normally in there? If so, say something to Parker."

"Pass me a fork, please, Parker," Jett whispered through

his teeth. It was a relief to finally take some action, even something so little. He was grateful that she didn't question him and that Ivan didn't notice, especially since he didn't actually have any food and thus had no need for a fork.

Valentine hummed in his ear. "Julia's here. When we get Anton, she'll take all of you to the *Starlight*."

Do we have a plan? Jett wanted to ask, but he couldn't think of a way to phrase it in a way that made sense. Asking for forks only went so far. Next to him, Ivan nodded sagely in agreement to something Dr. Tyler-Duke said in her presentation.

His presence was putting Jett on edge. He grabbed the nearest glass and took a sip, and then promptly spit it back. He didn't know what it was, but he imagined the raw appetizer would taste better.

The overhead lights were already off, so when the spotlights shut off the room was plunged into darkness. The only light was the glow of the fire, pacing back and forth in its water-filled prison. A murmur went through the crowd, but nobody was panicking yet. It was part of the presentation, Jett heard people whispering. Dr. Tyler-Duke stopped her speech, and she and her scientists could be seen whispering together, outlined against the orange flames.

"Are the lights supposed to be off?" Jett whispered. The room was full of low talking, and he hoped he was blending in.

"All of them?" asked Valentine.

"All of them," Jett clarified.

The lights didn't come back and the speech didn't continue,

and people in the room began to panic. A security officer took the microphone and encouraged everyone to stay calm and remain in their seats, but both orders were being disobeyed. The room buzzed with angry, scared, and confused voices like a discordant beehive.

The earpiece crackled, but instead of Valentine he heard Ivan Koswitch say "Greetings." He jumped and looked at the chair beside him, but it was empty. Ivan had disappeared.

"Ivan?" he said cautiously, pressing his fingers against the earpiece. "How did you get Valentine's radio? Where are you?"

"As I am sure you have noticed, I am not in ze banquet hall anymore," his voice answered. "I borrowed zis lovely radio from your friend. He ran, but he will not escape. No Head of ze Space Agency will escape. I have a plan, and my plans are always, let us say, well executed."

Another familiar voice joined Ivan's over the earpiece. "Hello, Jesse King."

"Teddy?" he exclaimed. He stood up and spun around, watching the tension grow. "This is all you and Ivan, isn't it? You locked these people in here. Why?"

"You're about to watch the demise of the Space Agency," Johnson gloated. "While they sat in their offices or at their parties, my colony suffered from starvation. You've seen the Red Planet with your own eyes, so you know the terrifying secrets of space - but do you see anyone in that room who cares? Anyone there who would dare go to space themselves?" The room was getting louder. Jett pushed the earpiece in further to hear Johnson speak. "I hate to see you die with them, but it can't be helped. We were actually friends, once upon a time. As the Rekans say, *spokoinoi nochi* - goodnight, Mr. King."

The radio crackled and went quiet. "Johnson?" Jett said. "Hello? Johnson!" No response. He ripped the earpiece out and turned to his friends. "We need to get out of here. Ivan and Johnson are here and they're up to something!"

"Look, are those Rekans?" Parker asked, pointing to the front of the room.

Several men with dark beards and hollow eyes stepped onto the platform, illuminated by the light of the fire. One of them snatched the microphone away from the Security officer, while the others took away the fire extinguishers the team was holding, and then they sent them into the audience with rough pushes.

The Rekan with the microphone mockingly shouted "long live ze Space Agency!" before throwing it into the fire. The Rekans disappeared through the stage door, shutting it before Security could catch them.

The room was still drowning in noise. "This is an outrage!" a man was shouting. "I demand the lights get turned back on before I sue for emotional damage!"

There was a faint whir from above them and the next moment it was raining.

"What on earth?" Robbie exclaimed.

Jett looked up.

The house sprinklers had been activated.

Water sprinkled down, soaking the tablecloths and the appetizers and the flashy suits and gowns. Now people were well and truly panicking. It was very clear that they hadn't intended on having their fancy clothes ruined, and that they weren't pleased about it. They jumped off of their chairs, shouting and yelling, many of them threatening the SA Heads and demanding an explanation. Out of the corner of his eye Jett saw an orange light grow bright.

"Jett! The fire!" Parker shouted.

The fire leapt to life. It didn't need much to feed on, Jett remembered; just a trace of moisture. It lunged off of the table and over the safety panels, chasing the rain. It danced and skipped and spread through the room, rushing over tables and chasing the soaking guests.

There was a mass exodus toward the main doors. The security officers beat against the heavy oak, shouting, and fumbled with their radios, calling for help. The Agriculture team was bravely grabbing guests and pushing them under tables, yelling for everyone to find a dry spot to hide. Robbie darted towards the back, but came back only a few moments later.

"The dishroom is locked, too," he panted. The hairstyle that Julia had worked so hard on had been reduced to a wet, sopping mess sticking to his forehead. "There's no way outta here, Jett!"

The fire rushed in their direction. Jett dragged Robbie under the table where Cariss and Parker were already hiding. There was a small circle around them of dry carpet where the table had shielded it. The fire narrowly missed them, leaving behind wet, sticky air.

"We're all wet," Robbie said. "Johnson's gonna burn everyone in this room!"

"I calculate that unless the doors are opened within the next five minutes, everyone in here will die," said Cariss.

"Thanks, Cariss," Parker said, "that's exactly what we wanted to hear!"

People ran and screamed. At this point the security officers were panicking just as much as the guests. Jett scrambled back into the rain. "Robbie, show me all the ways out. We gotta break down a door or something!"

Robbie climbed out after him. "All of the doors have intricate locks triggered by fingerprints or badges that we can't possibly get through, except for the dishroom."

"Then let's go there."

"This way," Robbie said, jogging on the soggy carpet. They pushed through broken chairs and flipped tables, and reached the other side of the room in record time. Robbie pushed aside a heavy curtain and hit his fist against wood. "Here it is!"

Jett leaned down to study the doorknob. "If I had time I could pick the lock."

Robbie glanced over his shoulder and shook his head. "I don't think we have time!"

"Okay. Let's break it down on one, two, three..."

They threw their combined weight against the door. Pain jolted up Jett's side and he staggered back, and Robbie clutched at his shoulder. The door hadn't budged.

"This isn't going to work," Jett reasoned. "I need a hair pin or a paperclip, and something bigger, like a screwdriver. Hurry!"

A wave of heat crashed over him and he jumped out of the way, rolling onto the wet carpet. The fire slapped against the door, burning away a layer of moisture and leaving it slightly blackened. The heat was unbearable for a moment but the flames danced away, licking the rain. He sat up, dazed. A man in a bowtie was next to him on the floor, cradling his hand that had been lightly burned. "I'm gonna sue," he wailed.

Jett pulled himself up and grabbed the doorknob, but he jerked his hand back with a sharp cry. The metal was blazing hot. He held his hand to his chest, half-tempted to wail dramatically like the bowtie man in the corner. He felt somebody bump against him and he turned to see Robbie, holding out a hair clip.

"This is from a wig I found on the floor," he said. He fumbled in his pocket and pulled out a small wrench. "And I know I'm wearing a suit, but that doesn't mean I'm not prepared."

Jett took the tools and knelt in front of the door. The knob was still hot but it was cooling quickly. He tugged on the hairclip, pulling it straight, and then bent the very edge. With his left hand, he put the wrench into the lock, and with his right hand he inserted the pin.

"Hurry, Jett," Robbie urged. "I don't think these people understand how the fire works. They've turned over most of the tables, so there are hardly any dry spots left."

Jett blocked out the chaos around him. He focused on sliding the pin back and forth, feeling the inner workings of the lock. "Hold the wrench," he said, handing it to Robbie. "Keep slight pressure on the edge of the lock. I'm hurrying. This takes a lot of concentration."

The noises and flashes of the room faded into the background of his mind. He scooted the pin, painfully slowly, and felt the faintest of movements. He slid it some more, closing his eyes and letting his fingers and his sense of touch take over. He felt a few *clicks*.

He pulled the pin out and took the wrench from Robbie, giving it a quick twist. The door swung open. The dishroom lay before them, and to his joy there were no sprinklers in it. The room was empty, and wonderfully, gloriously, dry.

"There's a door in here that leads outside. It should be unlocked," Robbie said, pushing in.

"Careful!" Jett called after him. "Keep an eye out for the Rekans!" He turned to the rest of the room. "There's an open door here! This door is open!"

His cry was quickly echoed among the cowering, wet guests. There was a chaotic, uncoordinated rush for the kitchen. A woman held up her pink skirts, tripping in her heels, her tears mingling with the rain. An elderly man clutched a handkerchief to his face, shaking with coughs, and struggled to the door. Jett held it open as the people surged through.

Fire lunged at the dishroom and everyone scattered, but they quickly regrouped as the fire fell back and Jett grabbed the door again. A man shouted for his wife, and another man clutched his tattered leather shoes and his shattered gold watch. A woman in a pantsuit collapsed and people rushed over and around her, until Parker stopped and dragged her out.

Robbie was on the other end of the dishroom, holding open the door that led outside. A gust of wind blew in, sharp and cold and smelling of trash and the sea, and it felt like heaven to Jett.

"Get outside," he directed people as they rushed by. "You're still wet, so hurry before the fire follows! Get out there and we'll close the doors."

Two middle-aged men struggled to get through first and it made Jett feel sick. After them, Dr. Moon appeared, supporting a woman that Jett guessed was his wife and followed by a teenage boy. "Thank you, King," he said as he went by. "Let me get my family outside. I'll be back to help."

There were still a few people left when the fire danced towards Jett. He looked at the trail of puddles that had been tracked into the kitchen. "Hurry!" he shouted to the stragglers. "I gotta close the door, hurry!"

The last few people stumbled in, with Cariss bringing up the rear. "Is that everyone?" Jett asked, searching the shadows of the banquet hall.

"That's everyone, yes. Close the door!" Cariss said, and he didn't hesitate to obey. He slammed it shut, and even through the door he felt waves of hot, wet heat as the fire fumed against it.

Dr. Moon and Robbie hurried over. "Come on, Mr. King. You saved us all," Dr. Moon said, pulling him away from the door.

Jett was achingly hot, and numbly he wondered when he had gotten the fresh burns covering his hands and arms. His eyes hurt when he blinked. Then he remembered something, and almost forgot about his pain. "Guys, guys," he said hoarsely, "Valentine's in danger. Johnson and Ivan got his radio somehow. He had just told me that Duke has Anton."

Dr. Moon pulled him outside and Robbie shut the door. It was raining, like it always seemed to be in this city. They were next to the outdoor pavilion where the press conference had been held earlier, the one they had watched on TV in the Valentines' home. It had a concrete floor, open sides and a high, sloping roof.

Wet and scared people huddled under it, while some were still fleeing, fueled by adrenaline. A business-looking woman in a pencil skirt sat on the concrete, cradling a man's head in her lap. On a bench, a young woman rocked back and forth. A man was pacing the pavilion, clutching a phone to his ear while water dripped from his cashmere suit. Parker knelt by an older man, helping him sit as he struggled to breathe.

Jett sagged, and Robbie and Moon struggled to hold him up. "Give me a moment," he mumbled. They helped him sit on the edge of the pavilion, where his head was dry but rain dropped onto his shoes. He looked down at his hands. Burn marks were seared onto his skin like red stains on a white cloth. On one of them, the skin was cracked and his fingers were curled up like legs on a dead spider.

Something stirred inside him, and whether it was anger or justice he didn't know. "Where's Johnson?" he asked hoarsely.

"He's probably gone," Dr. Moon surmised. "If he did this, he and Ivan probably fled immediately to avoid getting arrested. I don't think there's any chance we could catch them ourselves."

"You're probably right." Jett rubbed his eyes and glanced over his shoulder. "Is your family okay?"

"They're okay," Moon said softly.

Dr. Moon being gentle was just as odd as Valentine being sincere. Jett almost felt hysterical enough to laugh.

"Duke is still in there somewhere," Robbie said, worriedly.

"And Valentine," said Moon.

"And Anton," Jett said.

Wailing sirens and flashing lights approached, surrounding the pavilion. Security guards ran in and out of the complex. Jett stood up, wincing as the rain stung his hands.

23

Answers at Last

Earlier, before the chaos in the banquet hall had begun, Duke led Anton through the complex. It was disturbingly empty. He lifted his watch and considered calling his mother, but decided against it. He knew something was wrong but he didn't know *what,* and she was in the middle of the presentation and most likely wouldn't appreciate being interrupted.

They turned a corner and were faced with a door. "That's the room behind the stage," Duke explained. "We can get into the banquet hall through there and find out what's going on."

He hurried to push it open, but just as quickly he slammed it shut. His eyes flared.

"What is it?" Anton asked.

"Rekans," Duke said. "They saw me. Run!"

They dashed down the corridor like runaway freight trains. Duke scrolled down the contact list on his watch frantically, wondering who it was best to tell about the Rekans infiltrating the complex. His train of thought screeched to a halt when they turned a corner and found themselves face to face with Teddy Johnson and Ivan Koswitch.

The four of them hesitated at opposite ends of the hallway, four points to an oddly mismatched square. Ivan looked at Anton with interest, Anton looked at Johnson with hope, Johnson looked at Duke with anger. Duke looked at all three of them, and felt his chances of getting away unharmed steadily sink.

Ivan raised his brows, pocketing the radio in his hand. He took a step closer. "I zought you were locked up in Channyng's office, boy."

But Anton was oblivious to his presence. "Mr. Johnson!" he exclaimed. He reached into his pocket, pulling out a watch, and Duke mentally berated himself for never checking to see if the boy had it. Anton smiled proudly. "I am so glad to have found you, sir! I have your watch!"

Johnson held up a pistol, leveling it at Duke. "Don't move," he snarled. "Step away from him, Anton. Ivan, do you have any need for this scoundrel?"

"He is Nova Atlantis swine," Ivan answered. "We have no need of zose."

The corner of Johnson's mouth tugged up. "Well, Mr. Tyler-Duke, you die here, a traitor to every side. I have dreamed of this ever since you destroyed my colony and tried to take time and eternity away from me."

"Time and eternity were never yours," Duke said.

"Quiet!" Johnson shouted. He steadied his pistol. "How is your claim to time-travel any better than mine, you worthless scum? The only regret I have in killing you is that I'm doing enemies and friends alike a favor. We have all seen how your crimes outweigh mine!"

Anton stepped into the wide space between them and

held his hands up imploringly, still holding the watch. "Mr. Johnson, please do not shoot him!" he begged.

Duke's eyes widened and Johnson's eyes darkened, but Anton held his ground like a wall between their chaotic forces. The desperation on his face was the same as it had been that day on Reka, on the front steps of the Communications Center, when he had thrown a wrench into yet another tumultuous situation.

"What is zis? A traitor on our side as well?" Ivan said with a heavy frown.

Anton looked down the barrel of Johnson's gun and swallowed. "It will not work, Mr. Johnson," he pointed out. "Wemember when you shot him on Weka? It did not make a difference. I do not zink zat pistols can kill him."

Johnson snorted. "Does that mean I can't try?"

"I will not let you," Anton said.

Johnson lowered the gun by a fraction. "Why, you little skunk!" he shouted, losing his temper. "What's the matter with you? I raised you to be loyal to me, and not two-faced scum!"

"I do not zink it is necessary, sir, to kill him, sir," Anton stammered. "Mr. Johnson, can you not do zis one zing for me? Next time I will do what you say. I will do anyzing you want, sir, if you leave him alive."

"Zere isn't going to be a next time," Ivan said primly. "You are coming wif me, boy."

Johnson flinched. The gun lowered a few more inches.

"You are leaving me?" exclaimed Anton, bewildered. His hand with the watch twitched.

"Don't look at me like that!" Johnson demanded. "It wasn't

my choice, boy. This was the only way to get out of prison and pay off my debts. Look here, if anybody should be unhappy it's me. Ivan took advantage of me at my lowest!"

"We do not have time for zis," Ivan said, shifting from one foot to the other. "Zis place will be swarming wif Security in minutes. Johnson, shoot ze man and take your watch so I can take ze boy and go!"

"Do not let him take me!" Anton pleaded, moving towards them. "I will do what you say, sir. I will shoot Mr. Duke myself! I will do it! I will shoot him if you will not leave me!"

"Don't make it harder on me, boy," Johnson said. He swallowed. "Give me the watch, then go with Ivan like a good kid."

Anton hesitated, and then stepped back, clutching the watch to his chest. "No, sir! I zink I will keep it!"

They heard footsteps and voices. Duke watched the stalemate, willing the footsteps to move faster.

Ivan was seething like a pot boiling over. "Zis is ridiculous," he said. "Anton, come here at once."

Johnson lowered his gun until the barrel was aimed at the carpet. "Anton, you know I wouldn't leave you if I had a choice. You know you're the only thing I've ever cared about."

"Zat is a lie," Anton spat. He lifted the watch. "If you want ze only zing you've ever cared about, come and fight me for it!"

The footsteps and voices grew louder, nearing the corner behind Duke and Anton.

Johnson dropped the gun and lunged at Anton, right as Security officers poured into the corridor. Ivan turned tail and fled. Duke whipped his own pistol out and fired after him; Ivan dodged it and vanished around the corner.

On the floor, Johnson wrenched the watch from Anton's hand. He staggered to his feet and the watch whirred into action; in a flash he was gone. Duke winced as the time distortion seared through his head.

"What's going on here?" a Security officer demanded.

"Get Ivan," Duke ordered. "And see what's happening in the banquet hall. Go!"

They obviously recognized him for who he was and hurried to obey. Duke reached down and pulled Anton to his feet. The boy's face was bloodless, making his eyes stand out like stones in the snow.

"Are you okay?" Duke asked.

"I zink so," the boy shivered.

"Duke! Anton! What's going on?"

They looked up and saw Valentine running toward them, without his hands in his pockets for once.

Duke opened his mouth to answer, but then his throat went dry. Behind Valentine was his wife - the same woman Duke had seen dead on the space station ten years ago.

Anger surged through his veins like an old friend.

"Why is she alive?" he demanded. "What *actually* happened to the space station?"

Valentine held his hands out, palms up. "Come on, Mr. Duke, it was a little mistake."

"I've killed men for less!" Duke shouted, shaking his pistol. "You're a time-traveler. You must have done something that day that turned me into the same thing! What did you do?"

"He did it for me!" Julia cried, pushing her way between them. "Yes, I'm Dr. Addison! He was trying to save me. What happened to you was an accident!"

"Get your wife out the way," Duke snarled. "This is between me and you."

"We don't have time for this," Julia pleaded. "Our friends could be in danger!"

"She's right," Valentine said. "Ivan stole my radio. I was on my way to find Jett."

"Nobody is going anywhere until I understand what happened!" Duke shouted.

Valentine looked like he was going to continue arguing, but then something in his face shifted. Gently, he pushed Julia aside. Then he swaggered forward, his hands in his pockets and his head held high. "I created a paradox," he said frankly. "Everything you said you did when the station exploded is true. You went inside, you were in the explosion, and you died. I don't know why you remember it, because I used time-travel to undo it and I brought you back."

"Why?" Duke demanded. He tried to keep the fire in his voice, but a different emotion was quickly catching up with him and tears stung his eyes. "I lost my job and my mother because of that, and everything I ever had. I don't want these powers."

"I saved your life."

"I would have rather died!" he said. "Tell me why you did it!"

"I did it for my wife, and I'd do it again," he said. "She was an undercover agent on that station, not a scientist like your father. The SA has weapons in space, just like all the rumors say, and she and other agents were on that station with a stash. One of the agents turned out to be a fraud and things went down. From what I can tell, a fight started, and Julia and your father died. And then you walked in."

"And then what?" Duke demanded.

"One of the weapons was set off. We still don't know why. The place exploded and you all were dead. The moment I heard what had happened, I traveled back in time to save her, and I got there before Julia died but not in time to stop the explosion."

"But she was dead when I came in," Duke said, his voice wavering.

"I undid that, don't you get it? You both died. The place exploded and you were nothing but a million little pieces in space. But I time-traveled to get her out before it happened, and on my way out I ran into you. At the moment I didn't know whether you were supposed to be dead or not, so I panicked and saved you. I didn't think anything of it; I didn't realize you would remember dying instead of remembering me saving you. I created some form of a paradox."

"Time fights against those."

"It does, doesn't it?" Valentine said. "Nothing happened to Julia, but you walked away with your own time-traveling powers. I don't know why. I've kept an eye on you, but I've also kept my distance. You changed that day; Channyng took control of your life and now you're nothing but an empty shell of what you were before."

"Because you had to meddle with time!"

Valentine smiled softly, and it was infinitely more genuine

than any of the ones he gave to the public. "The things we do for love, yeah?"

Duke trembled and pressed his lips together. He lowered his hand, dropping the gun to his side. The fire in his eyes died down, replaced by black coals.

"Bring Anton to the *Starlight*," he said. "And then take your wife and go home. Before I change my mind."

"Bless you," Julia murmured, grabbing Anton's hand. They headed toward the lobby doors, but Valentine lingered behind.

"You'll see me again," he said. "Our ways will part for a while, but we will see each other again."

Duke pointed at the door. Valentine flashed his shark-like grin and ran.

24

To Freeze A Moment

Left alone, Duke tried every door to the banquet hall. None of them opened. Then he remembered the dishroom, and he ran outside.

He was not prepared for what he saw.

Wailing sirens and flashing lights.

A girl from Health and Safety with chapped lips and raw skin.

The Head of Engineering, struggling to breathe.

A reporter who loved writing about the Tyler-Dukes, unconscious on the concrete.

Dr. Moon's son, wiping blood from his mother's face.

One of his mother's assistants, crying over the phone.

Duke's steps faltered. He saw Parker, crouched next to an ambassador, helping him with a water bottle. Robbie and Dr. Moon were at the edge of the pavilion, and Jett stood between them with cracked and bloody hands. Security officers bumped Duke on their way past him, rushing to control the situation.

"Duke!" Jett exclaimed, pushing through the rush of officers. "Duke, where's Anton?"

"Valentine's taking him to the *Starlight*," Duke said, looking at the pavilion distractedly. "He's fine, don't worry."

"He's taking him *where?*" a new voice asked.

Duke turned and saw Channyng. His vicuña suit was wet and torn and his eyes were bloodshot.

Duke shuddered at the sight. "Anton's on his way out of here," he said. "I let him go because you had no right to keep him."

"Duke!" called Cariss. She emerged from the crowd and pushed into their little circle. "Jett, go sit down. We'll call you if we need you," she said, before turning to Duke again. "The Rekans locked the doors and let your mother's fire out. The banquet hall is destroyed."

Jett left. Duke clenched and unclenched his fists, and felt hopelessly, helplessly, weak. He looked up at Channyng.

"I quit," he said.

"Brandon, let's be reasonable here," Channyng said, and this time Duke recognized his tone for the manipulation it was. "It's really not a good time to send in your resignation when our guests look like they've been through a toaster. This is when I'm gonna need you most, man. We're a team."

"We're not a team," Duke said. "We're not friends or co-workers, either, or any of the other names that you've come up with. I was a wretched fool, and you're the man who took advantage of that."

Channyng sighed. "I'm gonna help you through this bout

of anger. That's what friends do. Let's go take care of this mess."

"Didn't you hear anything I said?" Duke exclaimed, frustrated.

"I did, but for your sake I'll overlook it," the man said earnestly. "Everything you have, you owe it to me. Just look in the mirror and you'll see you could never survive without me protecting you and your secrets. Look, someone just tried to destroy the complex. Let's not let them get away with it, okay?"

"This is your mess," Duke said bitterly. "You cheat and threaten everyone, and you've made people hate the SA so much that they're willing to destroy it."

"You don't mean that."

"As far back as I can remember, I just wanted to be useful. Turns out I just got used," Duke went on. "I'm leaving. I'm taking Jett and his friends back to Nebraska, and it'll be a good thing if I never see you again."

Channyng looked sorrier than he ever had. "You know I can't let you get away with that," he said softly.

He pulled a gun from his suit and fired at Duke with all the desperation of a man whose last plan had failed. The laser hit him and he cried out, falling to his knees. Cariss reached to intervene.

Another gun fired, and Channyng groaned and slumped into the mud.

Through eyes hazy with pain, Duke saw Jett, sitting on the edge of the concrete and holding the gun in question. He dropped the stolen weapon and held up his hands as Security guards swarmed around him. The crowd in the pavilion didn't even react.

Though his side was burning, Duke reached for Channyng. "You shot him!" he exclaimed. Frantically he searched for a pulse.

"I'm sorry, Duke, I'm sorry," said Jett, as Security hauled him to his feet. "He was going to kill you!"

"He can't kill me, and he knew it!"

"It sure looked like he was going to try!"

Dropping Channyng's wrist, Duke stood and glared at the Security guards. His eyes were a raging inferno. "Let him go!" he commanded, and they stopped in their tracks. "You know who I am: Brandon Tyler-Duke, the President's PA. What I say goes. You have far bigger things to worry about than this man, so leave him be for now. Take Channyng away."

There wasn't even any hesitation. The guards let go of Jett and crowded around the President's body.

"Thanks," Jett said shakily.

Duke barely heard him. "Where's my mother? Dr. Tyler-Duke, did she get out?" he asked. His eyes strained to find her frizzled hair and clipboard in the crowded pavilion.

"I... I don't know," Jett confessed. "I haven't seen her."

"I don't think she came out," Cariss said.

The words hit him like a brick. He recoiled, and then he turned and practically flew over the few yards that separated him from the complex. He sought out the door to the dish-room. Jett ran with him, while Cariss and Security and the pavilion fell back and out of mind.

Duke stopped in front of the door. "I'm going to do the thing Valentine showed me on Rendova," he said.

"You mean the thing that made you scream and almost knocked you out?" Jett asked, concerned.

Duke nodded and his eyes flickered. "It's just looking back in time. It should be easy." His hands began to glow. He felt himself start to time-travel, and he willed himself to slow down. His head ached, and he had the nauseating feeling of his organs being squeezed. He watched the flashing lights of the emergency vehicles around him fade, along with the crowd under the pavilion. He watched Robbie's vague outline take shape, holding the door in front of him open as people began to stream out.

He watched as each and every person walked out. Coworkers whose names he knew by heart, scientists he admired, the Agriculture team he envied and ambassadors he'd seen on TV. Dr. Moon came out with his family, and a moment later he ran back in. When he came back, he was supporting Jett and followed by Cariss. The door shut behind him.

He blinked and fell forward, catching himself against the kitchen door. The flashing lights and full pavilion came back in a snap, along with Jett, who was watching him worriedly. "You okay?" he asked.

Duke nodded, though his brain and his lungs were on fire. "It hurts... doing that," he panted. "I can't... do this kind of thing... anymore."

"Did you see her?" Jett asked.

Duke shook his head, using the door to stand up. He swayed, unsteady on his feet. "She didn't come out."

He grabbed the door and pushed it open. In the dark he could faintly see tiled floors, racks of dishes and a wall of automated machinery. Jett followed him in, shutting the door behind them. "You should stay out," Duke argued. "The fire is most likely still going. I don't want you to get hurt."

"I don't think you're invincible, either," Jett said. He grabbed the door that led into the banquet hall and opened it.

The room was still shrouded in darkness, dimly lit by flames that were currently running up the far wall, licking up beads of water. Shattered plates and glasses were spread over the spongy carpet. The sprinklers were still going, raining non stop, and Duke knew that the SA had a big enough water source to keep them going until someone finally shut them off.

He sprinted in and circled empty, fallen chairs and looked under fallen tables. Though he was still worried about his mother, it was an immense relief to see that Jett and Cariss had indeed helped the guests and the SA members to escape. As far as he could tell, the room was deserted.

He walked around the final table in the room and time itself seemed to freeze.

His mother lay face-up on the floor, staring lifelessly. Her blazer and scarf were singed, and her pin with the Space Agency insignia and the name *Tyler-Duke* clung stubbornly over her chest. Her skin was red and scarred, and the floor around her was warm.

Duke sank to his knees. Catching up with him, Jett slowed to a stop, staring at the body. He stepped back tentatively, wanting to give him a moment alone, but eyeing the fire with worry. Duke hardly noticed him.

Duke felt a strange disconnect to the situation, like he

was watching it happen to someone else. In the background, he heard Jett say, "Duke, your hands are glowing!" Looking down, he saw the familiar gold encircle his hands and tug him away.

His emotions controlled his power, pulling him back to the moments before his mother died. The empty banquet hall disappeared, replaced by what it had been in the not distant past. The silence broke. People ran around him, screaming. The fire flashed by. In the distance, Jett and Robbie were picking the lock.

His mother crouched under a table, gripping her clipboard. "Brandon?" she hissed. "There you are! Get under the table!"

"I'm a time-traveler," he blurted. "I have been since the space station exploded, but I never told you. And I love you."

She gave an incredulous laugh. "This is not the time to mess around!"

He blinked back tears. "I don't have time to explain. I'm not even supposed to be here. But I want you to know that I resigned, and I wish that I could've worked with you in Agriculture, and I love you."

"And you're a time-traveler," she said skeptically.

He gave a wet laugh. "Yes, I have all kinds of strange time-powers. Somebody told me I'm going to be known as the Man who froze time. Sounds rather neat, don't you think?"

"You can't freeze time, Brandon."

His eyes and his hands flickered and he felt something inside of him break free.

"Watch me," he whispered.

And just like that, time stopped moving.

The room became unearthly quiet. A table froze in place in the middle of being flipped over; the people around them turned into statues in various stages of running and jumping. Duke and his mother stood, unhindered by whatever power had frozen everything around them.

Beads of water from the sprinklers hung in the air like tiny, crystal balls. His mother's jaw dropped in awe, and she stepped farther into the stillness of the room. The fire towered above them, caught in the act of leaping high in the air, arched over the room like a delicate statue. Its light was reflected off of a million drops of rain in midair.

She stood under the fire, looking up with wondering eyes. "Brandon… what did you do?"

"I think I froze time," Duke said, as awed as she was. "Or at least I slowed it down. I've never done this before."

"But you have time-traveled before," she said, tearing her eyes away to look at him. "I saw you in the doorway when I started my speech, but then you left. Did you time-travel to be here now?"

He hung his head. "Yes," he admitted. "I should go back even further and stop all this from happening. I can rearrange this day to make it the day you wanted it to be!"

She huffed a laugh. "You just undo time as you please?"

"What's wrong with that?" he snapped. "It's fully within my power!"

"Your ability, maybe," she scoffed. "But as much as I wish this hadn't happened, nobody here has given you permission to rewrite their lives and take away their choices."

"Mother, you don't know what's about to happen!"

"No son of mine is going to run about using powers like

that willy-nilly," she continued. "I can't say that I approve of this time-travel nonsense. It seems a bit too much like playing god to me. You'd better go, and make sure you only use your powers for serious things from now on."

"Mother, I can't just leave you here!"

"What other choice do you have?" she demanded. "I'm scared, same as you. Though I'm glad to know that whatever happens to me, you have a way to get out."

Tears streamed down Duke's face. "I'm sorry if I ruined your reputation," he said.

"Oh, hush," she said. "Forget about my reputation. If anything happens, just take care of my legacy, will you?"

His hands started to glow. Dr. Tyler-Duke turned back to her invention, clutching her clipboard to her chest; the tower of fire arced above her, held back by his power. Small flames had branched out, wrapped around beads of water. "It's never looked better," she said. For a moment she was not just a renowned scientist, but also a mother. "It always made me think of your eyes. You know you're special to me, right?"

Before Duke could answer, the room broke free from his hold and water and fire came crashing down. The glow on his hands spread, and within a second he had shifted in time. The noise and the chaos disappeared, and he was back in an empty room with Jett hovering behind him.

His legs were jelly and his head was swimming. Time distortion pounded against his temples. Somehow he managed to kneel beside his mother's body, and he unpinned the Space Agency pin on her blazer. The insignia and the name *Tyler-Duke* stared back at him solemnly. He closed his fist around it, and then the pain overwhelmed him and he fell into the waiting arms of unconsciousness.

25

Angel, Nebraska

Duke woke up in Cariss' house. She had a little room above her garage that he had stayed in before, during his time in Nebraska. He was in a familiar bed with a blue quilt, and across the room from him was an aquarium with boring looking fish, right where it always had been.

He sat up. In horror he realized his hands were empty, but he relaxed when he saw his mother's pin on the nightstand beside him. It lay next to a potted plant that wasn't usually there.

He heard a noise in the hallway. "Cariss?" he called, uncertain.

She peeked her head in. An emotion most resembling relief crossed her face, but she schooled it away. "You've been out for almost twelve hours," she said.

"How on earth did I get back to Nebraska?"

"Have some faith in me. You passed out, so I got everyone to the *Starlight*. I got one final jump through time out of it, and here we are, the twenty-first century."

"Thank you," he said, leaning back against the pillows. "I'm sorry I fainted. I think I pushed myself too far."

She nodded, and then gestured at the potted plant with her chin. "Dr. Emmett and Tate stopped by and left the weed as a thank you, or maybe a get-well gift, I don't know. They heard you liked plants."

He raised his brows. "Really?"

"Yes. Also, Jett King is in my living room. Are you well enough for me to let him in?"

"I think so," he said, pushing the quilt aside. He found he was still in his dress pants and shirt, but his feet were bare. "Where are my shoes?"

"I threw them away," Cariss said over her shoulder as she walked out. "They were wet and smelled like smoke. Your jacket, too."

"You know those were my only shoes in this century, right?" he called after her.

Moments later Jett walked in. He gave a little wave with a hand wrapped in white bandages. "I'm glad you're okay," he said. He saw the potted plant and his nose scrunched. "Oh, no, they got you some ugly weed, didn't they?"

"I like it," Duke assured him.

"Cariss told us you liked plants," Jett said. "She also said you used to work in your mother's department. You know, I've got cousins who work for county agriculture, as well as the farm bureau. I could probably get you a job."

Duke blinked. "What?"

"I mean… if you're staying," Jett said. "We sort of assumed you didn't want to go back. The SA was too busy to worry about you when we left, but how long is that going to last? When they sort things out I don't think you'll end up in a favorable light."

Duke ran his hand through his hair. "I'm not going back to Nova Atlantis anytime soon. But I can't stay here."

Jett's face fell. "Why not?"

"I'm the only one who can find Johnson," Duke pointed out. "And besides that, why would I stay? I only ever came here because Channyng told me to. I'd like to put an end to that storyline."

There was a *boom* outside the window and Duke jumped.

"It's fireworks," Jett explained. "Cariss lives close to the Millers' field, and every Fourth of July the town goes out there and we do a barbecue, stay up late and light off fireworks. I was out there with my son, actually, but I came to see if you'd woken up yet. You and Cariss are welcome to join us."

"I don't think I will, but thank you," Duke said.

"Alright. I'd better get back out there before they wonder where I went," said Jett. "If you change your mind, we're all out there. And don't leave town without saying goodbye to all of us first, okay?"

"Oh!" said Duke. "I... I'll probably leave sometime next week. I have a few things to take care of before I go. You can ask the others if they want to come say goodbye. Next week. If they want."

Jett smiled. "I'll tell them. You'd better tell Cariss to prepare for company."

"Company?" he echoed.

Jett paused, halfway out the door. "Yeah, company," he said. He counted on bandaged fingers. "Dr. Emmett, Tate, Anton, Parker, Robbie, and me. Is that enough of a party for you? We'll bring the food. Knowing Parker it's bound to be something amazing. Sound good?"

"That's.. yes," Duke said. "It sounds great, thank you. A little change of subject here, but I'm really sorry about betraying you guys and taking Anton."

"You brought him back. It's water under the bridge," Jett said good-naturedly.

Boom. Boom. Boom.

Duke saw flashes through the lace curtains this time. He hadn't spent enough time in Nebraska to know who the Millers were, but he had seen the field behind Cariss' house before. He imagined it littered with picnic blankets and the remains of a barbecue, with children laughing and watching fireworks light up the evening sky. Despite the noise, it sounded peaceful. His eyes dimmed and he wondered when he had last had any peace.

"You can come if you want," Jett said, watching his expression.

He shook the idea away. "I'm good here. Thank you for everything, King."

"Don't worry about it. See you sometime next week. Oh, and Cariss told us that you like chess, so expect Tate to bring a set and make you play with him, whether you're both concussed and bedridden or not."

A smile sprang to Duke's face, unbidden. "I look forward to it."

Jett grinned and walked out. Duke turned to the plant on the nightstand, studying the leaves and trying to narrow down what it could be. His eyes flickered merrily. *This is the first gift I've been given in a very long time*, he thought.

He jumped when Cariss cleared her throat. She had slipped into the room unnoticed, and stood with her arms folded, frowning at him with gray, piercing eyes.

"It's a philodendron," he announced, nodding at the plant and feeling almost giddy. "I think it's a rugosum. I have one back at my house."

She looked entirely unimpressed.

"I'll give it well drained soil, not too much sun," he continued, "and it'll grow quite a bit more than this."

"Duke," she interrupted. "I've been thinking about the frankly disturbing things you said to me as we left Rendova."

The color drained from his face.

Cariss narrowed her gaze. "Who did you kill?"

THE END

Notes

What is Angel's Crypt? Whose side is Valentine really on? What does the future look like for Nova Atlantis? Will trouble follow them back to Nebraska? And can Duke find a way to save Jett from dying?

Rendova isn't the end of the story. This book is the second in the *Paradox* Series, which follows the adventures of eight main characters: Jett King, Robbie Finley, Parker Quinn, Duke, Dr. Emmett, Cariss, and the twins, Anton and Tate.

Characters in order of appearance:

Brandon Tyler-Duke (usually called Duke; works at the Space Agency; from book 1)

Dr. Tyler-Duke (Duke's mother; Head of Agriculture)

President L.A. Channyng (President of the Space Agency; Duke's boss)

Dr. Julia Addison/Valentine (Undercover agent; Security officer; Valentine's wife)

Ernest Valentine (Head of Public Relations; leader of the anti-Nova Atlantis movement)

Dr. Moon (Head of Health and Safety; member of the anti-Nova Atlantis movement)

Dr. Simons (Head of Communications; murdered by Channyng)

Jesse (Jett) King (police officer from Angel, NE; former friend of Johnson; from book 1)

Parker Quinn (friend of Duke's; aspiring artist from Georgia; from book 1)

Thomas (Tate) Emmett (paradox twin from Angel, NE; from book 1)

Cariss Swusterlinn (friend of Duke's; member of the anti-Nova Atlantis movement; from book 1)

Dr. Ronald Emmett (relative of Jett's; doctor from Angel, NE; from book 1)

Robert (Robbie) Juno Finley (pilot of the *Starlight*; from book 1)

Anton Venedict (paradox twin from Reka II; nicknamed Myshka; from book 1)

Teddy Reka Johnson (former president of Reka; from book 1)

Ivan Koswitch (former vice president of Reka; member of the Space Agency; from book 1)

www.ingramcontent.com/pod-product-compliance
Lightning Source LLC
Chambersburg PA
CBHW070753160726
48004CB00001B/170